The Sun-tanned Lemmings or Spring Vacation

This is a story about the twenty thousand hot-blooded collegians who descend on Lauderdale each spring with every gland going berserk. For three wild and wacky weeks they whoop it up in a whirl of sand and sun, tan and fun—forsaking the pursuit of learning for the pursuit of the opposite sex.

Tune in on Merrit, the well-stacked Midwest coed: "I hereby announce that the sex in this book will be found exclusively on pp. 16-17, 41, 110-114, 160, 163-165, 199, 242-248, and 311. Also pp. 74-78 and 219 and 331. . . .

"If you are deeply concerned about such crucial topics as The Influence of Walt Disney on Religion, Large Families, Education, Virginity, The High IQ, Faith, The Luck of Henry Thoreau, Stimulation, How Society Makes It Tough for Kids, etc. . . . buy this book.

"I want *serious* readers, not a bunch of BB-stackers."

THIS IS A REPRINT OF THE HARDCOVER EDITION
ORIGINALLY PUBLISHED BY RANDOM HOUSE, INC.

where the boys are

Glendon Swarthout

A SIGNET BOOK

Published by THE NEW AMERICAN LIBRARY

Published as a SIGNET BOOK
By Arrangement with Random House, Inc.

FIRST PRINTING, DECEMBER, 1960

SIGNET BOOKS are published by
The New American Library of World Literature, Inc.
501 Madison Avenue, New York 22, New York

PRINTED IN THE UNITED STATES OF AMERICA

to Miles, my son: ***bon voyage!***

This is
a story,
and any
resemblance to
real kids
or a
real U,
living or
dead, is
not only
coincidental but
fantastic.

1

Life is like a long blind date. The Social Chairman of a boys' dorm calls the Social Chairman of a girls' dorm and says he needs some flesh for Friday night, no foul balls, nothing too brainy, all queens and amenable, can she supply? And she says yes, she can, but what about the boys, the girls will want vital data and stuff. To which he snorts what for, they'll be *seminal*, and hangs up. You are some of the flesh supplied. You wonder what the boy will be like, what will happen on the date, where you'll go, what you'll do, will it be great or the all-time fall-through, and Friday night you tear around like wild getting ready to be beautiful. The buzzer rings. You make an entrance and meet him. You go somewhere and do something. Maybe you have a real ball, maybe it's hell, maybe both. But no matter what, before you can really know each other, you and life or you and your date, you've mingled or said no and it's over. Tuggle and I did a dance because the pavement was burning our bare feet with our arms full of beach towels and tan oil, etc. The thing was, we couldn't cross Atlantic Boulevard for the traffic, so we waited until about a thousand cars passed packed with tourists staring at us in our swim suits and finally we made it and ran till our feet hit sand and there we were and there everything was!

All that Atlantic honest-to-john Ocean and genuine ships sailing on it and sky and sunshine and actual palm trees and miles of true beach and thousands of wonderful live-it-up kids!

In my entire life I had never been as way far out.

You may be very sophisticated and have been to Florida before but let me clue you. I'd never seen the ocean before or ships or palm trees except in movies and magazines. Neither had Tuggle. I'd never been further south in the winter than Indianapolis to visit my aunt. Our Senior Trip in high school was supposed to be to Washington D.C. on the train but two hoody boys in our class put on a race one night with their cars full of kids and smashed up and the school board made a large odor; you know how things are in a small town; and canceled the trip. The semicolons in the preceding sentence are probably wrong. Frankly, my big mechanical trouble is semicolons. Our English teacher was always telling us dashes were a sloppy piece of punctuation and to save them until we really needed them with the result that I am still saving them for hell knows what and trying to make do with semicolons. When I am old I shall mourn not for a misspent youth but a whole slew of unspent dashes. So don't plan on too much in this, punctuationally at least.

Anyway. Here we were, Tuggle and I, after nearly two thousand miles, with everything about to begin, and I want to describe it in detail. I am fairly sharp at description. First, the ocean. If you come from the Midwest and have never seen it you are really clutched, that is, seized by an emotion. The finest thing about the ocean is that it isn't *illimitable*. At the horizon it simply stops. To me it proved what I've been made to prove, that the world is flat. Gads, think what we could do with edges! Line up the generals and admirals from everywhere and forward march. Inform our congressmen and cabinet members and the pols of all countries in fact that they are going to be in a parade. Build the loveliest drag strip in history and put our hot-rodders on it. With no strain we could drop into infinity overaged movie stars, Greek shipping tycoons, the complete cast of the Mickey Mouse Club, the premiers of Russian satellites, Texas oil men, presidents and faculties of state universities, missile countdowners and button-pushers, football coaches, Madame Chiang Kai-shek, the men who made cereal and deodorant and cigarette commercials for TV, South American dictators, sports writers, Bing Crosby's boys, and all the assorted scourges of the world. Let's face it, the globe would be much more interesting and convenient flat. Plus I think it would be good for men to know they have *limits*. The ocean was like an enormous fat man with a bland face. Once in a while he would open his mouth in a wave and grin foam. There were ships sailing to and from romantic places like Cuba and Port-au-Prince and Galveston and coming over the water, if you listened creatively, you could hear the sounds of gourds and voodoo drums and steel bands, though from Cuba it might have been firing since it seemed to me I'd read they were putting on a revolution. It's difficult to keep up on current events in college because there isn't time and also because they're so damn current. The sky was as blue as the sea. Above were small clouds clipped and haughty as poodles being led along on leashes. An airplane putzed past trailing a sign which read "Go, Man, Go, To Pokey's!" But the really fabulous thing was the beach. Wide and sloping, it was like a white and endless Band-Aid protecting the land from the ocean, except that the sun changed the white to gold and there on the gold, sitting, lying, standing, walking, as far as we could see, about twenty lucky thousand of them, were the prospectors.

Grinning at each other as though we had at last aced life itself, Tuggle and I joined them.

If you enroll at any school in the U.S. east of the Mississippi you hear very soon about spring vacation in Florida. Everyone goes who can afford it and whose folks will let them. If you never go you are really out of it. Spring vacations at most schools coincide, falling the last weeks of March or the first weeks of April, halfway through second semester or just as winter term ends. Anyway, from all over the Midwest and East they blast off for Lauderdale by plane, train and bus but mostly by the carload. I'm not sure why they started coming to Lauderdale but *Life* has even done a picture story on the whole deal. So now it's a tradition.

Why do they come to Florida?

Physically, to get a tan. The weather up north is simply unknown that time of year; snow and slush and cold and Gothic; the perfect climate for exams and suicides. Also, they are pooped. Many have mono.

Psychologically, to get away. They have just finished mid-semesters or finals and they have personal problems to escape from or try to solve and besides, what else is there to do except go home and further foul up the parent-child relationship? Another thing, they need to recuperate from our new national disease, peopleosis, which is to the spirit what mono is to the student body. For example, at the U, where Tuggle and I go, the enrollment is about twenty thousand and most of us live in dorms. Everyone has a number. Mine is 181226. In our dorm, dear old East Swander; named after Eliza Hickok Swander who was the first woman prof at the school and back around 1870 or 1900 invented a spray to protect snap beans from the black blight or something and also left a swad of money to the U as the result of picking up a lot of prime real estate adjacent to campus; there are a thousand girls divided into eighteen precincts, or cell blocks, and hutched three to a room in rooms designed for two, which enables alma mater to pay off the mortgage on the dorm faster. Three girls to two desks and two closets and one phone buzzer and one window and you begin to be as claustrophobic as the clown walled up alive in "The Cask of Amontillado." How can you have solitude? How can you have dignity? You cannot even contemplate in the bique. Perpetual buddy-buddy is enough to make anyone a misanthrope. But the most spastic thing about East Swander is that you have to maturate simultaneously with a thousand other girls while every species of adult yammers at you to get the show on the road. With their proverbs and hard-knocks diplomas and homilies on conduct parents can be dismal enough, but profs, tossing out a challenge per lecture, are the absolute bottom. To them students are rats which can be trained to jump at certain doors for food and ideas. Once trained, change the symbol on the door from a Cadillac or a cross to Piltdown man or other-direction and see what the little rodents do. Our noses become so bloody from banging on the wrong doors that if we react at all it's reflex. Sure, sometimes we wait till class is over and give a secret leap in our souls but in general we are responsed out. As I said, here are all these girls having to *become* instead of *be,* with all the attendant tears and rashes and flashes, which I assume is also true of the boys in their dorms. What you have then is twenty thousand kids running in relays the gauntlet of growth. Living in this is like being in the belly of a pregnant pig, with the whole wriggling litter squealing to be born, while outside, in the pen, society kicks hell out of the poor sow to speed up the process.

Biologically, they come to Florida to check the talent. By that I mean to inspect and select. When a *Time* reporter asked one girl why she migrated she said because "this is where the boys are." You've seen those movie travelogues of the beaches on the Pribilof Islands up by Alaska where the seals tool in once a year from the Bay of Fundy or someplace to pair off and reproduce. The beach at Lauderdale has a similar function. Not that reproduction occurs, of course, but when you attract thousands of kids to one place there is apt to be a smattering of sexual activity. And the terrific thing is that many of the boys are from the Ivy League: Harvard, Princeton, Yale, etc. A lot of them go to Bermuda and Nassau to snob around with girls from Eastern schools but the intelligent ones, having heard about Midwestern girls, tear down here to see if it's true. So if you are a girl and want to meet the authentic Ivy League article; and who doesn't; Lauderdale is where to go.

It took Tuggle and me a long time to find spreading room for our towels but finally we did and began oiling each other and observing. We were stuck, unfortunately, amid a pride of girls, a real Amazonia. I had never been so conscious of female flesh. Let's face it, American girls today are big; busted and footed and hipped and shouldered and bottomed. A group of them in tight swim suits looks like a football squad in shape for a two-hour scrimmage. Had the Sabine women been stacked on their scale there'd have been no Rome. Of course I may be generalizing to justify myself. I am five-nine in heels and I weigh in at one thirty-six. My statistics are 37-28-38. I wear an eight and a half B shoe. I may not be feminine but I am damn ample. We all are. It is ridiculous nowadays for girls to strain to be seductive. Companies go on advertising creams and mists and gossamer underthings when what we should really be in the market for is stuff like electric razors and Charles Atlas courses and jock straps, etc.

Incidently, my name is Merrit.

And speaking of flesh, it is time I said something about sex. This is not going to be one of those Riviera-go-rounds by smutty little girls. What's immoral about them is that they don't enjoy *either* writing or bedding. Or one of those campus comedies in which the kids listen to jazz all day and mattress all night and never go to class. Most kids *do* go to class. But I admit sex is very important in a book today. You watch the people in a bookstore or by the paperbacks in a drug store, turning the pages with that bored yet hunting expression. They are not looking for literature. If I'm anything, it's realistic. To be read you have to heat it up. So if this book is ever published and you are someday browsing around in a bookstore or drug store I hereby announce that the sex in it will be found exclusively on pp. 16–17, 41, 110–114, 160, 163–165, 199, 242–248, and 311. Also pp. 74–78 and 219 and 331. So if sex is what you happen to be interested in you may turn at once to these pages and save your money but if you are deeply concerned about such crucial topics as The Influence of Walt Disney on Religion, Large Families, Education, Virginity, The High IQ, Faith, The Luck of Henry Thoreau, Stimulation, How

Society Makes It Tough for Kids, Love, etc., and a slew more, and would also like to read an account of what is probably the most gallant and selfless and inspirational deed ever attempted by young people, at least in this era, buy the book.

I want *serious* readers, not a bunch of BB-stackers.

2

Weight yourself 1,2,3,4: During an evening discussion with intimate friends, you are more interested when you talk about the meaning of life, literature, developments in science, social amelioration.

ALTGELD INREACH-OUTREACH TEST

"Dr. Edelson," I said, "I'm not sure what 'amelioration' means."

"Betterment."

"Thanks. By the way, Doctor, what are 'inreach' and 'outreach'?"

"A definition at this point would not, I think, be particularly helpful."

"I still can't answer this one."

"Why not?"

"Because when I'm with intimate friends we don't talk about any of these."

"What do you talk about?"

I grinned. He paled.

"Do the best you can."

I slapped down the pencil. For two awful hours he had kept me hunched over a table weighting and circling while he rubbed his receding hairline and hitched up his white socks. I suspect any man who wears white socks.

"Doctor, why do I have to take these?" I begged. "I only wanted a little advice about next term."

"My dear young lady. Testing is a service provided by the University. We administer a complete battery of tests, depending on whether the problem is personal or academic. I should hazard a guess yours is both."

"I'm bored with having my hand held," I said. "We aren't allowed to do anything for ourselves, not even to make a mistake. How ever did the pioneers swing it?"

"The Counseling Clinic processes three thousand students yearly."

"That's because you're *here*!"

"And so are you!"

"I wouldn't be if you weren't!"

He shot up, then down again. He had a very short fuse.

"My-dear-young-lady-do-you-mind-finishing!"

I groaned and took the pencil. My War With American Higher Education began almost as soon as I arrived on campus. All students at the U are dual-enrolled when they are freshmen; which I am; and which does about the same thing for them that dual exhausts do for cars. There is a one-year program of general education called the Core College. This means you have to take a reading and writing course called Core Language and one called Core Science and one on how to live effectively called Core Living. At the same time you are enrolled in whatever other school you elect. I picked Elementary Education for fall term. That is the chic thing these days. But when it was too late to get out I lost my illusions so had to wait until winter term before I could switch to Home Economics. But this, too, turned out tragically, I was trapped again and it would soon be spring term and my freshman year would be over. It is absolutely hell in this world to have no *major*. So my latest Enrollment Advisor; three others had already sloughed me by transferring me to somebody else; referred me to the Counseling Clinic and here I was, being serviced, rammed into an office with a weedy Ed.D. in Testing who had thrown the Manne-Previn Personality Prognosis and the Bobb Temperament Totalizator at me. And now this Altgeld job. When I weighted the last question, something about who had contributed more to civilization, Aristotle or Marx or Satchel Paige, I handed it over to Dr. Edelson and sat giving birth to a headache while he scored it.

"How did I do, Doctor?"

To my shock he extended another test. "There are two more. It would be unscientific of me to conclude anything until we have a total picture."

That did it. We went round and round. I demanded to know something about my outreach. He gave me some abracadabra about taking the complete battery. I told him he was covering up his inability to read *thing one* from my scores. He insulted me by saying they were so chaotic and traumatic it was his clinical judgment there was nothing else I could be spring term except an Uncom.

"I won't be an Uncom!"

"Why not?"

We came out of our chairs like cobras out of baskets.

"Because no one has the right in these times to be uncommitted! Because I will not take a free ride on the world!"

He sprang hypertensively upon his desk and tore off his shoes! "Instead of leading cheers in high school why didn't you decide what to be?"

"You don't believe in your own tests!"

Now he was taking off his white socks! "You and your problems! My car needs a valve grind! My kid needs braces on his teeth!"

There were his bare feet and he was shaking a can of powder all over them!

"Dr. Edelson, what in God's name are you doing?"

Powder billowed up in clouds!

"What in God's name does it look like? You make them itch! Students make them itch! The only thing wrong with education is students!"

My own were on fire! I grabbed my books and ran for the door!

That is how it is. Ask if it's raining out and you're "referred" to the Weather Bureau. Ask the way to the Ladies Room and you're "processed." Freedom of choice, my backside. Try to choose and you are so delved and tested and prognosed, etc., that you take the easiest way out. We do not maturate; we get more scores. Liberty depends on electricity. Whatever will we do if they cut the current? This is also what I meant about coming down to Florida to escape or solve a problem. Mine was simple: What To Do With My Life. Bobb and Altgeld had been no help. Dr. Edelson had his own feet to powder. It was my baby. But I had scads of confidence, I was eighteen years old and in great shape. And one of the best things about the kids on the beach was that they were so *casual*, not like seals barking around or birds busily making guano, just talking and reading papers and listening to portables and playing bridge and saying hi to the sun through every pore.

Tuggle and I baked a while on both sides when something made us sit up. Down the beach about a block kids were jumping up and clearing a path. Someone was doing what dynamite couldn't have done. As the path opened toward us almost Biblically we saw who and why. Tapping ahead with a white cane was a blind boy. He was fantastically tall and skinny and wore only a pith helmet and dark glasses and droopy swim trunks. Nearer he came, tentative and bony, then turned around, cross-legged down on the end of my towel and said:

"Peel me."

Frankly, I don't know how to introduce a character. Should you describe him physically or use dialogue to let him out of the kiln? And when someone as unbelievable as TV Thompson taps into your book it's really rough to be verisimilitudinous. For example, one of the first things he did was take off the dark clips from his shell-rims. Blind, he was not! He also removed his pith helmet and moaned with pleasure as I eased a great swatch from his back. He had one of those tenderized skins which never tans but burns and peels, burns and peels in cycles. He was from Jackson, Michigan. "The slogan of which," he said, "is Jackson, The City of Action."

We exchanged data. He was twenty, a junior at Michigan State, a communications major, working his way through, and why he was called TV was a secret known but to God. When we asked what about the blind bit he said one of the most charitable things you can do for people is to let them be charitable. "For example, I was sitting around late in this radio and TV station one Sunday night reading the papers and there was an article about Barbara Hutton and her third divorce. She said she was very unhappy because she had led a tragic life. It ticked me off. So I wrote her a post card saying Dear Miss Hutton, you and your goddam tragic life, with all your collateral what have you got to bitch about? Here I am, a kid about to graduate from high school who can't even swing one year's college tuition. The kick was, on my way home from the station I mailed the card. I hadn't planned to, I just wrote it to get a catharsis of the emotions, but I did." He had a large mouth which assumed all kinds of shapes and as he talked his huge hands dipped and soared like birds. What had once been a crew-cut had grown out to sort of a thatched roof. "A month later comes this letter from some secretary saying Miss Hutton has been touched by my note and hopes the enclosed will enable me to enter college. The enclosed is a check for twenty-five hundred. I was going anyway so I bought a car, a year-old Porsche, a real bomb."

"I don't believe it," I said.

He looked very hurt. "I never give skin to anyone who isn't basically *sincere*." He put on his dark glasses and helmet and stood up, which meant arranging his ribs and tibias vertically, and said he had to cut the scene, he would check us in the afternoon. Then using the white cane he cut a swath through about three hundred sympathetic kids. I had anyway finished his peel job.

Tuggle thought he was cute in an ugly way. Her passions have round heels. She has a terrific mind, though.

Myself, I crossed him off as one of those fraudy types who sometimes con their way onto campuses. The Mike Todd of Michigan State. Only with a very vulnerable covering.

Around noon we went back to the apartment, put on skirts and blouses, walked to a malt shop for something foodlike, found ourselves gaped at, the malt shop deserted, caught on, and feeling real gauche whipped back to the apartment and put on our swim suits. According to Maxine and Susy the routine in Lauderdale is: never eat lunch if it costs and to be seen by daylight in anything but a swim suit is very déclassé. We had arrived last night half dead from driving thirty-six straight hours in an old car and after much bad news finally located this apartment. The manager said it rented for twenty dollars a day during the season but we could have it for ten and though this was more than Tuggle and I could afford we went so ape over having our own apartment we said okay and moved the two suitcases right in. It was a living room-bedroom-kitchen-bath on the second floor of a small new building called the Shalimar which was right beside the Bahia-Mar Yacht Basin with all the sailboats and cruisers anchored. Our veranda overhung a swimming pool, terrace and palm trees. Walk into a paradise like that at night when you are flaked out from school and snow and the road and you will pay any fantastic price, even ten dollars a day. The thing about money is that most of the kids in Lauderdale are very underfinanced. I say most because we became involved with two real exceptions. But this is why eating except just enough to sustain life is out and why paying such high rent was fraught with fiscal peril for Tuggle and me. After $20 for our ride down and return and all the rent we each had a nut of $25 for food, entertainment, tan oil, post cards, souvenirs, and a luxurious tropical existence. Meanwhile, back at the Shalimar, across the pool from our digs, two boys from Illinois and two from Wisconsin shared a one-bedroom. In another; we never did find out just which one; were three more who actually went to *Yale*, believe it or not. So the Shalimar was loaded with talent and in that respect a bargain. The other apartments were crawling with tourists, including next door to us a couple from Long Island, New York, whose name was Petworth. Underneath us in an efficiency, which meant sofa-bed and wall-kitchen, were two low-budget girls: Maxine, who was fairly fat but smiley and motherly, and Susy, a little intense blonde who wore glasses but had a cute figure. By coincidence they went to Michigan State so we right away asked them if they had heard of an oddball named TV Thompson.

"You mean the Mike Todd of Michigan State?"

In between laughing they gave us the scoop. In his lemon Porsche convertible he had hit the student body like a flu epidemic and the administration as staggeringly as a losing football season. He had paid for his first year from the sale of faked ID or identification cards so kids under twenty-one could buy liquor and his sophomore year by getting up an inter-dormitory radio station which provided music for studying and between records oblique references to local dry cleaners and pizza places. The center of his empire, his dorm room, was reputed to be as frenetic and entrepreneurial as the head office of A. T. & T. He aced his courses without buying books. He was elected president of the freshman class and impeached for rigging the election. Ditto the sophomore class. Whenever the school was about to toss him he solidified himself with the Dean of Students in some way like breaking up a pantie raid on the girls' dorms by delivering an impassioned address on responsible citizenship to the nylon-maddened mob of boys. Why he was called TV they did not know. But the legend about Barbara Hutton was undoubtedly true, plus anything else he might have told us. Bag up in one flesh Norman Vincent Peale and Manolete and Ann Landers and J. Paul Getty and Mort Sahl and Juan Perón and Ed Sullivan and Mickey Cohen and Bishop Sheen and other such wheeler-dealers and big-time operators and you would have TV Thompson.

Incidently, he wore a homburg to classes.

Well, we talked with them about schools and stuff. They were fun kids though somewhat on the teachery side since that was what they planned to be and I guessed they had come to Lauderdale for whatever kicks.

"I've even started smoking!" Susy choked. "I don't inhale, though."

Maxine grinned. "Next it'll be drinking and worse."

We asked if they had made any progress with the Illinois and Wisconsin boys and they said they were working on it.

"What about the Yale boys?"

"You can dream about the essentials," Maxine said. "You know, like rubies and chinchilla. But a date with a real Leaguer would be too much."

Susy's eyes watered from smoke or despair. "I mean, if I could have one I'd be ready to die."

The four of us sat around in hopeless silence. Maxine was right. You have to be practical. There are probably a few things too *great* to aspire to. Finally I said chins up, the Ivy League experience might happen to any of us, but the only way it could was to put our nickels in the deus-ex-slotmachina and pull the lever so let's off to the beach.

By now, having got to Florida a day earlier, they had a swell start on tans but Tuggle and I were just crisping well when along came TV Thompson, good as his word. This time he skipped the blind dodge, stretching his long legs over bodies and swinging his white cane like a swagger stick. We introduced him to Maxine and Susy and they discussed kids and profs they had known at Michigan State until Tuggle; whose only failing is that she is so obvious around boys; asked how he was raising tuition this year.

"Tests," he said.

"Tests?"

"Personality. I run a service." TV's hands took off. "You know, companies start interviewing seniors the winter of their last year and they all line up in their best suits and fresh brush-cuts. Recruiting brains today is so big it's damn near a matter of logistics. But, and here's the kick, they don't want brains. A high IQ is worse than bad breath. Grades count, sure, and activities, but the clincher is the personality. So they give these seniors a test to take home to fill out and tell them what the company is most interested in is how well a guy will groove, how well he'll adjust to the job and the togetherness; in other words, can he disappear without a trace into a department. The poor joker takes the test to his dorm or house and stares at it scared witless his personality will turn out to be dominant or off-beat or something. He's so tied up he doesn't dare lift a pencil! After much sweat he calls us."

"Who?" Susy asked.

"Thompson Testing Service."
"What for?" Maxine asked.
"To take the test for him."
"Why?" Tuggle asked.
"Because I know what the company wants."
"What?" I asked.
"Nothing."
"Nothing!" we cried.

"You win, pledges." TV pushed up his shell-rims. "The perfect corporate character today is the mean, the average, the norm, the absolute in-the-middle nothing. The problem was to find one. I did, a guy in our dorm, a real human zero. You've heard the song, 'Out of the night, when the pale moon is bright, comes a horseman known as Zero.' The only difference is, this guy rides a bike. His personality is so minus, put him in an airtight room and he would not even use up the oxygen. Write to him care of General Delivery, he will never have an address, except you would never write to him. This is the kind of unknown guy the exact instant he was conceived both his parents sneezed."

The other girls were dying laughing and could hardly ask what about him.

"Basic. We call him in, pay him ten bucks, and with his invisible pencil he carves in that test the mark of Zero. The senior takes it back to the recruiter in the morning."

"After paying how much?" I asked.

"A mere bill. One hundred."

"I think it's shocking," I said. "In fact, it's dishonest."

"*Au contraire,* babyroo. The company has what it wants, a personality so plastic they can extrude it into any shape, no genius or fox or aberrant, and the happy senior has what he wants, a great starting salary, a George Nelson desk, and a junior executive button."

"What if he turns out to be an individual?"

"Bingo, they have a president." He all at once stood up, put on his dark clips, took my hand and said, "Let's bolt, babyroo."

We walked through and around the prones and supines and halfway up the beach I realized I was having my first *date* in Florida! But by the time we reached Atlantic Boulevard I was neither grateful nor flattered. My first date should have been special because I had been looking forward to it for such aeons but here I was tagging along barefoot and sunburned with a strange physical and ethical character going and doing Lord knew where or what. He took my arm helplessly and signaling with his white cane propelled us right out into the traffic as six lanes of cars smoked rubber braking to a halt so the blind boy and his girl-pal could cross.

"TV," I said, stopping in the middle of the street, "every thing you do is tricky."

He faced it. "You don't condemn me. You condemn society."

We might have had a hot debate but cars, suspecting something, laid on their horns and we went on across to the Sand Crab.

I have not mentioned anything except my dimensions. I am *not* plain. I am probably, however, one of those girls about whom people say well, she has a nice smile. My hair is bear brown and uncurly and when a month ago I realize how much of my youth and strength I was wasting putting it up every night that I could have devoted to something significant like studying or the United Nations I said the hell with it, all is vanity saith the preacher, and had it bobbed straight across the back and sides. I am philosophically opposed to tinting or peroxiding. My eyes are blue. I wear no make-up except lipstick. My mouth is okay. I do have very good teeth.

The Sand Crab is so famous you hear about it at school. It is a beer bar with a capacity of about thirty kids packed noon to midnight by about two hundred with an infinite capacity. There are no tables, no booths, just stools around the circular bar and the biggest feat is getting through the door. Once you're in, if you have to go to the bique, plan on a burst bladder. Beers were passed overhand to us. My impression of the décor was that it was sweaty and smoky and the chest of the boy behind me, who was loud and from Penn State, was hairy. TV had set out alone from Michigan State in his Porsche. I asked him why alone and he said he had reached a crucial juncture in his career and needed to do a lot of ratiocinating. When I pressed him about his crucial juncture he evaded the issue by getting us more beer. "A thing on the way down," he said, resting his drinking elbow on my shoulder. "A semiadventure I haven't been able to sublimate. Outside Knoxville at night there was this hitchhiker and I'd promised myself isolation. But he stood there in my headlights too proud to thumb. All he had was a sign on his suitcase. Havana. That stopped me. We took turns driving and talked all night. He was very sharp, a Phi Bete from Minnesota and about to graduate this June. But you know where he was going? Miami to Havana to Santiago to be in on the revolution! Think what he was giving up, a degree in three months, a suburban future, the works, just to go to Cuba and shoot up the sugar cane fighting for a country not even his own and possibly be killed! How many kids at the U do you know would do a thing like that? He'd given away all his clothes, packed one bag and taken off with no message to the school or his parents. I really rebutted this character, I argued with him all the way to the airport in Miami, which is where I dropped him, but he took the ball on downs. I can't shake that crazy guy. He's been raising hell with my Id or something ever since." Being about to slug the boy from Penn State who was toying indecently with me only to find it was now a girl fumbling for a cigarette, I asked why. "Merrit," he said, using my name for the first time, "Merrit, what he was doing, and I use the word with great care, was . . ." He shook his head.

"Was what?"

"I'm scared to use it. I never have before."

"Live dangerously."

"Okay. What he was doing was *epic*."

I looked away. So did he. Language like that, considering these times and conditions, can be worse than dangerous. It can be embarrassing.

"TV," I said, "do you believe in God?"

"I believe," he said, "in Walt Disney."

"You too!"

We had clicked. It was an idea each of us thought unique to himself. To celebrate, TV ordered more beers.

I should say something about the grape. I drink. I didn't in high school because getting plowed then was not so much alcohol as the *will* to get plowed, which bored me. To spend all that money and then have to put out most of the effort yourself seemed to me sort of futile. But I drink only when in the right mood and do not have to be pressury or artificial about it. If I am warned it's *de rigueur* I become belligerent and will not touch a drop. The important thing about drinking is this: it's *not* important. Poetry is bigger than proof. Man's soul is more subject to cirrhosis than his liver. So don't make a king-size, self-conscious, existentialist deal out of it.

TV was telling me how it happened to him. "Like most kids, when I was little I thought of God as a bearded old buddy. I prayed for everything. Then when I was fifteen and got a job at this TV-radio station in Jackson I spent every minute I could staring at those monitors. We had no set at home."

"People forget," I said, "how much more contact kids today have with Walt Disney than they have with church."

"Sure. Saturation. After two or three years a kid is bound to switch images. A mustache is a lot easier to live with than a beard. God awes. Walt smiles. He forgives you your sins as you forgive him his commercials. Your folks give you a bad time. Walt's always nice and his explanations of things are simple. No, you can lose with God but you can't with Walt."

We drank thoughtfully.

I said, "I got onto it after Disneyland was built way out in California and Walt started plugging it on his shows. I guess I was trying to imagine what heaven might be like and all I could visualize was a beautiful, enormous, sanitary amusement park where kids wanted to go more than anywhere else in this world or out of it."

"Divided into four areas. Adventureland, Frontierland, Fantasyland, Tomorrowland."

"You could spend a really swell eternity," I said, "never being bored, just walking around the park being entertained by a gang of talented, self-assured teen-agers."

"What about hell?"

"I don't know. I don't think anyone believes in hell any more."

"I don't either. God has mellowed too much to operate one."

"If there is a hell," I said, "it must be a nice big room with a terrific color set on which you never get a clear picture."

Besides getting the good out of the beer now, TV and I had established a rapport. I no longer distrusted him completely. He had a fine imagination, a great sense of humor, and his thinking, at least on the subject of Disney, was sound. We were at last at the bar and there was air space for his hands to zoom and dive. I asked him if his nickname developed out of working at the TV-radio station and he took evasive action by telling me about his career. At first he shelved records and emptied spittoons, etc., but it being discovered he had a wild line of chatter he was soon given his own dee-jay show every night from nine to twelve, called "Thompson's Turntable." By now he was ordering beers on schedule and also potato chips. Each time he would take a dollar bill from the webbing of his pith helmet, telling the bartender to keep the coins. It had been a strange adolescence, circumscribed by the size of a monitor screen yet at the same time limited only by the length of the coaxial cable. But on a crazy diet of platters and tapes the young ninth-grader throve. The station became his home, audio and video his father and mother, and those formative years had given him his goal.

"What?"

"Communication."

I didn't get it.

"Babyroo, we are so overpopulated that nobody can reach anybody else so nobody knows what the hell transpires. It's as though everyone on earth has lost the power of speech except the ones with a mike or a camera. The mass media men have the last set of vocal chords in the world and they will soon run the show because any sound, even a belch, is better than silence."

That was his ambition, he was practically certain of it, to command communication. Someday he would captain his own network, with a few movie studios as seed beds for series. When he so much as cleared his throat, seas would part and reactors explode. He would graduate in another year and tool straight to New York City. He had already written to the presidents of NBC, CBS and ABC.

"Why?"

"To let them know I'm coming."

I began to suspect him again even though my value system practically reeked of beer. Also, I was slightly ticked off at the prospects. Dates in Lauderdale were supposed to be fabulous; you wore heels and a swish dress and convertibled off to Miami Beach for a gay, mad whirl of night clubs, luxury hotels and costly drinks served in coconut shells or dugout canoes, etc. Either all this was apocryphal or possibly only on an Ivy League date. If you were stuck with Michigan State, even though he had a helmet loaded with money, you stingied around with potato chips and draft Budweiser. Beer tastes on a champagne budge. And got your charge out of rubbing the sand from each other's legs. It was *encouraging*, however, to be out with a boy whose feet were larger than mine. TV turned good listener and asked me all about my parents and home town and stuff. His mother had died so early he could not remember her and his father ran a punch press in a lawnmower factory and drank up most of his pay. He implied that most of his youth had been a struggle to extricate himself from his origins in the best Dickensian tradition. Jackson High was very class-conscious and he had never, despite his dee-jay show, been able to establish himself socially. When his hands began to lose altitude I knew it was time to take off. He agreed. We disembraced our legs and fought out of the Sand Crab and it was night. We were both really bulbed and I tagged after him through throngs of kids in swim suits buying post cards and girls looking at boys and boys looking at girls and waiting for come what might. TV really did have a darling yellow Porsche two-seater with the top down. We scrooged in and he gunned us away out Atlantic Boulevard. What kicks! I had never ridden in such a small bomb. The motor was in the rear, practically under yours, and when TV revved it the torque or whatever it was roared right up into your vitals. The cockpit as he called it was so small that he looked like a great skinny spider devouring the steering wheel. TV had a heavy foot but he drove surely because he loved his car.

We cruised north a couple of miles until he pulled over on a drive-out and parked. Gads, what beauty! It was mystic. Over us royal palms leaning and in front of us a magnitude of ocean under about a million stars and behind us the long strand of hotels and motels braceleting the boulevard with their lights. We had an herb. TV told me about his first job, when he was ten years old and had to earn because his father was such a sot. It was after school in a three-minute car wash. He was very small and as each car started down the line on the chain his duty was to open a door, scoot inside with the nozzle of a big electric vacuum cleaner and vacuum out the interior, then scoot out again and slam the door before the hot water hit the moving car. Sometimes, when he needed more money, he would play hooky from the fifth or sixth grade and work all day. If the truant officer came looking for him he would do a disappearing act into the steam and hide down in the pits with the white-wall scrubbers. All through junior high he had a perpetual cough and cold.

Suddenly he started the Porsche and one-wheeled around and across the boulevard into the court of an elegant motel and stopped and said to get out. I could not understand why until I walked with him to the center of the court. Like a great star sapphire lay the oval of a swimming pool. It was gorgeous. Two undersurface beams suffused the water so that it came alive with light.

"I've never been in a pool," I whispered.

"Neither have I."

That pool was a sort of symbol; for me of the glamour life no girl from Carter City would dream of having; for him of power and social status, etc.

We looked at each other, clasped hands, and jumped. Sensational! We came up tingling and blowing and his pith helmet floating and hauled ourselves up the ladder and stood dripping and grinning not from cold but from pride. And suddenly TV wrapped his infinite arms about twice around and kissed me and I let him and it was fun because of his rubbery lips.

"TV," I said, "straight-arrow. How come you invited me?"

"Basically *sincere*," he said.

I accepted it this time because I could understand how sincerity in a girl would bulk larger than any other quality with anyone so sharklike. For a minute we were shy.

"Pools have a *right* to be swum in!" he cried, his hands blasting off. "Let's put on a poolathon!"

He ran us back to the Porsche and down Atlantic to the next pool, which was in a swank hotel patio, and leading me by the hand took us into it with a mighty splash! And after we raced several laps it was kiss again, drip dry, smoke and away. We pool-hopped practically from one end of Lauderdale to the other, ovals, kidneys, rectangles, squares, and one Olympic-size, every one exotic and surrounded by palm trees with floodlights attached and tilted so that the light shafted up the graceful stems to the very fronds. I have never had such a chlorinated ball on a date.

During one stop I explained my problem. "Even if it havocs up my vacation I have to beat this thing," I said. "When I go back to register for spring term I have to declare myself. Home Ec and Education are out forever, I know that, and I absolutely refuse to be an Uncom."

"Why?"

"For one reason, because my folks are paying the shot and you know what college costs. For another, what a waste of time and taxes. Gads, TV, even a prostitute is committed to *something*. The biggest reason, though, is philosophical or in that area. I just think that with the world in such sad shape it is really reprehensible and cruddy not to have a goal, not to sign up for some branch of service, you know what I mean. It's like an elephant sweating and straining and finally giving birth to a nit."

To my chagrin he just stood there with his wet trunks at half-mast shaking his head. "I can't help, Merrit."

Then he said we had to break the spell so we went to the Porsche.

Eventually, how late it was I hadn't the faintest, we wandered around to the rear of one apartment to scout the pool only to find there was merely a terrace but the view was sublime. It was of the Bahia-Mar Yacht Basin and along the docks and catwalks were hundreds of yachts, their hulls and masts silvery as fish in the starlight. As we watched, a big motor cruiser, exhausts snorting, running lights on, glided through the basin toward the waterway which opened into the ocean. It was so lovely I had trouble swallowing.

"TV," I said, "what's your real first name?"

"Herbert."

"How old are you?"

"Twenty."

We watched the lights of the cruiser diminish. It was very dark and still on the terrace. Obviously no kids were staying here.

"That boat," he said. "All I can think of is, maybe it's going to Cuba. That mixed-up, epic guy from Minnesota is there by now. Maybe he's already dead."

We had a moment of silence.

"Merrit, I'll tell you why it's TV Thompson and I've never told anyone." For once his hands acted out not excitement but agony. It wasn't because of the station. His nil social life in high school started on the same high level his freshman year at Michigan State. He received no bids to pledge because he suspected fraternity men were jealous of his financial acumen and Porsche. The ostracism carried over to the distaff side. Sorority girls and popular independents breathed cold when he phoned. Finally, after two celibate terms he swung a date with a sorority queen and gave her a terrific evening, dinner, champagne, etc. She got very tight and while they were parked and making out she all at once said no and called him the Al Capone of the campus. He raped her. After he took her home he panicked. He was terrified she or her sorority would inform on him to the University Police. He was eighteen years old. So after a couple of Damoclean days he bought and had delivered to her house an $800 color TV console with his name on a card. It was not returned. He was not arrested. But from then on he was tabbed TV and boycotted.

He had not had a single date since. None of the boys in his dorm had buddied up to him either. He was *non campus mentis*. He had absolutely no group. To cap the climax he later learned that the queen had round heels for everyone else.

There were tears in my eyes. It was the most heart-rending story I had ever heard.

"So that's the score, Merrit," he said, holding his helmet and glasses, his head bowed. "Now you know. The only woman who's ever been nice to me is Barbara Hutton."

"Oh, TV," I tried to say, "I'm so dreadfully sorry!"

Then we went into a clinch so violent that we swayed and would have lurched into the yacht basin had he not directed us to the nearest piece of furniture, which was sort of a sun lounge, and we sat down still in the clinch. To be candid, we necked up a storm. Eventually, to be more effective, we lay down.

Well, class, we have reached a high or low point in this dissertation depending upon your attitudes toward nature and stuff. Those who wish may take notes. But first I would like to list a few extenuating factors:

1. I was flaked out from no sleep and the poolathon.
2. We had solitude.
3. Hunger. A girl cannot count on the calories in potato chips.
4. Beaucoup beers.
5. The sun lounge was very comfortable.
6. I was so sunburned my skin was extrasensory.
7. Huge surfs of sympathy washed over me.

In other words, we played house. That is a current euphemism. Afterward we put on our suit and trunks and stretched out sharing an herb. Our toes twined. "I'm sorry I couldn't help, Merrit," he said. "With your problem. I'm polishing one of my own. That's what I meant in the Sand Crab about a crucial juncture." He went on to say, almost to himself, that his dilemma had come up this last term. He had won out over both heredity and a lousy environment, wangled himself up to a plateau of achievement from which he could stare back upon what he had done and ahead at what he would do. As for the past he was not sure the end had justified the means. What scared him was how easy it really was to make money and high grades because it proved that if he were competitive and cynical and tricky enough he *could* actually command communication someday and he did not know if the utter bastard he would be by then ought to have so much power over people. So he had driven down to Lauderdale alone in his Porsche to think the matter through.

"Essentially, don't you have to decide what you really want?" I asked.

He nodded.

"Well, TV?"

He looked at the dark yachts as tied up and immobilized as he was. I heard his teeth grind.

"I want to make a mark on the world so deep and raw they can see it from other planets."

I sat bolt upright. "Herbert Thompson, that's awful!"

"Why?"

"Because it sounds like something out of *1984*! And you know it and that's why you're so schizoid!"

He cupped his chin. "I know it."

"Life," I said, "isn't a *promotion*."

With one hand I moused in the thatch of his head. "TV, what else might you like to be?"

"A catcher in the rye."

"Don't be trite."

"Okay." he took a deep breath. "Some kind of a damn saint. Except I don't trust myself."

"Why not?"

"O, I could wear a sackcloth and tear around some desert flagellating myself, I'm a red-hot showman. But simultaneously I'd have ropes up and shills buying tickets."

We brooded about it. I peeled away at his problem as though it were his back. I felt sorrier than ever for both Herbert and TV Thompson, so nervous and boy-man. For that was actually his trouble. He had a violent phrenia. The boy trying to vacuum the Orwellian interior of the man coming slowly but surely down the line on the chain and for his pains being whipped by the man, not paid. He was a morality play on wheels, with the motor in the back. So he had taken a few days off from free enterprise and driven alone to Florida to grow up. Of course, that's about all the time you have any more. As I reflected on it I really believed I could love this bony Barnum, so dear and demon-driven. He was like one of his own dee-jay records: on the front was the pop tune everyone bought and on the flip side was the sweet song no one had heard but me. Maturity is *much* tougher to commit than rape.

"TV," I said fondly, "you have so much on the ball that for the sake of society I hope you choose right."

"Maybe what I need is a good woman."

"Sincere."

We grinned at each other in the dark. Then we didn't grin. It might be fantastically true. Something in which he could believe, like the love of a nice girl, might water the plant of his immense potential for good. What a challenge! TV's fingers on my cheeks were like a child's. I about expired with tenderness and a sense of mission.

"Merrit, Merrit," he whispered, "could you love me?"

"Maybe I do," I sighed.

When TV drove me home he took off his pith helmet and kissed me almost spiritually on the forehead.

Something unspiritual was going on at the Shalimar. From the second-floor veranda I gazed upon a really sordid scene. Lounging around on chairs were three strange boys and lounging around on their laps was Susy. I did not recognize her at first without her glasses and her hair up in a tail but I did recognize Maxine, who sat at the other end of the pool trying to chaperone by remote control to no avail. The boys were in trunks and Susy in a swim suit and there were beer cans floating in the pool. I remembered Maxine saying next it would be drinking and worse, which was so right because those three weedy boys were sort of rotating little Miss Michigan State from lap to lap, necking and doing as much impure research as they could while she laughed abandonedly. She *is* majoring in Elementary Education, I thought, and if she carries on she will pick up the Pabst Blue Ribbon for sure.

Tuggle came out of deep sleep as soon as I turned on a light in our living room, which was furnished modernly; you know, walnut and foam-rubber cushions; J. C. Penney Danish; and wanted to hear all about my date. When I told her about the poolathon she said with all TV's loot it was chintzy of him not to at least give me a blast on Miami Beach. Before she became too interrogatory I asked about Susy and the strangers. She was checking her eyebrows.

"Leaguers," she said.

"Ivy?"

"The cream." She went into the bathroom and returned with tweezers and standing close to the mirror began to tweeze. "Yale, no less."

"No!"

"It's a fact."

"How can you be so calm?"

"I wasn't at first. They live right downstairs. I was invited. Yikes, my hair."

Tuggle had changed her hair so often in school, from brown to blonde to red to umber, plus peroxide streaks, that it did look a little motley.

"You said yes, I hope."

"O, I had a few cans with them until I got the picture. All they wanted was a count. You know the song, 'Hot hands I love, beside the Shal-i-mar.' And I was supposed to be privileged to participate."

I should define a count as being any time you are asked to a party and it turns out the only planned entertainment is to drink and wind up with your date in flagrante delicto.

"But Yale," I protested.

"Yale-male. They may call it New but it's the same Old Haven. A few beers and so to bed. If a girl from the provinces gets any fringe benefits such as culture she is expected to be grateful." Tuggle gave a savage tweeze. "Another illusion shot to hell."

I knew how hurt she was because I knew how high our hopes had been about meeting boys from Eastern schools and what might happen.

She turned. Her voice was low and shaky. "A year ago, a month ago, I'd have played lacrosse with them. But not now. I made a vow on the way down here, Mer. I promised myself to try for a man the chaste way. God and you know I've tried everything else. And so help me I'll keep it if I have to go to the local blacksmith and buy a belt!"

We sacked out in silence. She was near tears and there was certainly nothing appropriate I could say after my night. I thought tenderly of my basketball-built hero and lover, about the many points he had made with me, and about how, with the right girl to warn him against fouling, with his height and drive and imagination he could score among the very stars.

Incidently, I was *not* a virgin. My treasures, alas, had already been rifled, about which more later. Nor did I spend a sleepless night covered with guilt, shame and confusion. If parents think their daughters can attain young womanhood in 1958 in a state of pristinity they are really out to lunch. U.S.A. today stands for Universally Stimulated America. Sex has become a National Track and Field Meet and when it comes to championships conditioning tells and if you do not believe we are all damn well conditioned check the birth rate. What with movies and TV and plays and books and magazines, kids naturally walk around with hot palms. For example, in high school and college we read and discuss so much stuff about dating and marital adjustment that we have it on our minds so much that we go out and make every mistake in the book. What teachers give one-tenth as much time to Euripides? Or Botticelli? Or Manny Kant? I've been assigned reading in about ten different books by one woman anthropologist who found fame by making her first field trip to Polynesia or somewhere when she was twenty-three to study the interesting premarital customs of the natives, which was supposed to be a feat. What they don't realize is that *any* date in this decade is a field trip. I clue you in, a girl runs the entire range by the time she is eighteen. Myself, I have sort of classified boys as sweepers, strokers and subtles. Sweepers kiss you for a while and then attempt to take you bodily as they might a shock of wheat and reap the harvest. This is unsuccessful with me because I am as powerful as a pro tackle and throw a mean brush-block. Strokers involve you in amorous dalliance and then try to hand-pet you into a hypnotic state, using a clever caress-pattern on hips, thighs, and whatever else is convenient. They usually tune the car radio in on classical music, are well-read in physiology, and are dynamite if a girl has intellectual pretensions. Subtles are the most dangerous because their approaches are so unusual and various that a girl may become so interested in what is going on, that is, may project herself so completely into the drama, that ACT III is over before she knows it. For example, I dated one boy in high school who could weep buckets at the drop of a no. Unless you kept a cement heart until his ducts were drained, you were lost. Among the other offenses I have had thrown at me by subtles on Saturday night, beside the standard split-T and single-wing, are the father image, the naturalism of Rousseau, the ill-health-due-to-frustration, the suicidal, the historical; ranging from Hero and Leander to Grace Kelly and the monarch of Monte Carlo; the literary, including the Omar Khayyám or *ars-longa-vita-brevis-so-how-about-it-baby?*; and the coming of age in Samoa. I do not exaggerate. And I am neither the world's most-wanted woman nor a girl from a broken home. It would be difficult to play the femme fatale coming from Carter City, which is really not a city but a small Midwestern town with "Pop. 4000" according to a sign at the city limits. The slogan on the sign, which was erected by the Chamber of

Commerce, is "The Most Beautiful Little City In The World By A Dam Site." This is thought to be a knee-slapper and a good example of small-town humor. There *is* a dam which was used by a flour mill about a hundred years ago but all that remains is a picturesque millpond out of which, every few years, a small boy catches a big trout and has his photo taken with it and sent to the city papers because theoretically it's impossible for a trout to be in the pond in the first place. I know Carter City is not beautiful enough to brag about even though my frame of reference is limited but it is my home town and I love it and would be willing to spend many an old-fashioned Christmas there in later life. Of the two drug stores, my father owns one. He is a swell person, a graduate of U where he met my mother and she helped put him through the College of Pharmacy, and he served in the Navy in the Pacific in World War II. I have two brothers. The younger, who is twelve, we currently call "Have Gun" and the older, who is sixteen and going through the jalopy phase, we call "Will Travel." That is another thing on which I had better set the record straight so that what I write about my adventures will not be misconstrued. Also, in order to provide a healthy literary atmosphere. I did *not* have an unhappy childhood. My folks love each other and me and I love them and there is no strain. I have no traumas or psychoses or neuroses or complexes or obsessions and my Ego and Id and I function as a team. If this makes me less interesting, tough. But I would bet the most perfect peanut-butter-and-banana sandwich ever assembled that there are more well-adjusted people around today than people who aren't and I think it is damn tragic more of us do not appear in books.

3

symbiosis, n. Biol. *the living together of two species of organisms: a term usually restricted to cases in which the union of the two animals or plants is not disadvantageous to either . . .*

The American College Dictionary

I cannot seem to untoil myself from the subject of sex. But there is one more item on that particular agenda before we may go on to higher things and that is my attitude toward virginity. In my opinion it's ridiculous and picky of society to turn it into an *institution.* The whole deal is simply not that *monumental.* And I am not merely a poor loser either. All the yakking and controversy has forced me to change sides: my sympathies now extend to the *boys,* not the girls. As far as I'm concerned Marjorie Morningstar was as much a bag as Pamela. What with pimples and puberty boys have enough to endure without being terrorized about the sanctity of every so-called vestal in his neighborhood nor do I think a girl's misplacing it somewhere as catastrophic as The Decline and Fall of the Roman Empire. To hoard it for some bridegroom the way old ladies ball string always seemed to me miserly and cunning. Nevertheless, believe it or not, I stayed pure as the rose all through high school not because of a vitamin deficiency or the absence of the old rah-rah in the boys I dated but because of my philosophy. I made up my mind not to be seduced because that meant playing the role of victim, which I despise, in sex or life or anything else, so among the lads of Carter City High I soon became known as the Babe Didrikson of the Back Seat. A hundred times I fought the good fight and won. Then my attitude altered. What was mine was mine and I would damn well dispose of it any way I wanted but above all else I would have freedom of choice. You know by now how I feel about existence. If life was edible I would be The Fat Woman of the World. So one day; there were certain days on which I seemed to mature more than others; I came to a decision: I would give my maidenhood away to someone for the sheer exaltation of it. Furthermore, I would bestow it not upon any eleventh-grade Presley who was already a manytime winner but upon some sweet soul whose days might thereby be enriched and happier. So in the spring of my junior year I made a real bid to join the Deflorated Daughters of America. The boy eventually selected, whom I shall name Malcolm, was perfect for the purpose. He was goodlooks, shy, intelligent, almost never dated, played clarinet in the band, and came from a fine family in case there should be any malfunctioning. I invited him over one night to talk Shop, which is not a pun because junior girls were required to take a course called Shop in which they learned how to hammer nails and make lamps and stuff while the boys had to take Home in which they learned how to turn on stoves and boil water, etc. I suppose these courses were intended to make us more all-round domestically. In any case, Malcolm appeared trusting as a lamb, my folks were naturally out and my brothers asleep, and after exchanging pleasantries we soon settled down to more technical matters on the living-room divan. Malcolm made love with surprising savoir-faire, which might have been due to many hours of practice on the clarinet; I have heard trombone players are best because they develop a terrific lip; and when we were both breathing hard and I had given him every sign the supply was equal to the demand, to use economic terms, he inquired if I was a virgin and when I responded in the affirmative to my consternation he leaped up, righted his disarray, and in a spasm of boyish emotion swore that he would never, never be the one to send an innocent girl down the road to ruin. That damn boy was an *idealist!* Round and round we went, up the walls and over the furniture. I used every argument which had been employed upon me in the dark of night, I played Tschaikovsky's *Francesca da Rimini* on the hi-fi, I coaxed him into smoking a cigarette and slugging down a shot of my father's sloe gin, but to utterly no avail. Malcolm was a real nurd. In the end he said he was saving himself for marriage, and broke it up by leaving. I could have hit him with a lamp. In a perverted sense it was the most immoral, not to say humiliating, evening in my recollection.

Incidently, I did manage to make my gift to life eventually, about which more later.

It was the most beautiful right eye I had ever seen: deep, deep brown, almost black, and so steady and male that after a minute of gazing into it with my left eye I had to blink. The lashes of the eye were very lush. The profile was noble. The ear on my side fit the head perfectly and had a lovely lobe. The kind of crew-cut I abominate is the bristly job so short the scalp shows. His was just long enough to be soft and seductive. He was beginning to be too heavenly to be true. Then a well-shaped hand moved into my vision and the forefinger wrote slowly in the sand.

"?"

I smoothed it out to reply.

"Merrit"

"?"

"frosh"

"?"

"18"

"?"

"U . . . ?"

"Ryder"
"?"
"senior"
"?"
"21"
"?"
"Brown"

I nearly petrified! Brown! By some celestial coincidence your friend and mine, Merrit of the U, had been radared upon the beach in Fort Lauderdale, Florida, beside an Ivy Leaguer!

I should explain that Tuggle and I had slept late and come over around noon to put in more time on our tans. It was crowded as ever with happy ones. While she was making a fourth for bridge with two boys from Northwestern and a girl from Denison I lay waiting for TV to locate me as he said he would and dreaming of different methods, after we were married, to develop him into a great force for good when I happened to open my left eye.

We sat up simultaneously and had one of those horrible-wonderful moments when two human beings sort of gulp each other like malts. Even sitting down I could tell he was not tall; a little more than my height; but his build was dreamy, he took a tan well, and he was not overhirsute. His trunks were simple black nylon and from the way they hugged his waist you knew that on him Ivy League clothes would *belong*. In an unstriking, *casual* way he was the handsomest boy in my total experience. And one of the finest things about him was the way he onced me over. Most boys stare you stark naked with all the finesse they use to tear off a sweatsock. But his inspection was so oblique, so polite, so practically *disinterested* that it was as though he had said please allow me to remove your swim suit momentarily and I had replied but of course. It was complete, though. And when the wonderful-horrible moment was ended he gave me a slow smile featuring white, even teeth.

"Would you care to come over to The Sheikh's?"

I did not know where or what The Sheikh's was. But if he had said walk into the sea with me until we disappear forever in its briny depths I would have. I actually felt I was *in* a movie.

"Thank you," I said.

In order to cross Atlantic Boulevard he waited until the light changed, then took my arm.

The Sheikh's was the kind of suave place an Ivy Leaguer would prefer. Ten times as large as the Sand Crab, with walls of glass, wrought-iron chairs, low tables, and lizardy kids sprawling around getting as potted as tropical plants, it was decorated to represent an oriental interior. The ceiling was canopy-striped, there were murals of mosques and oases and belly-dancers on the walls, and the back part was a patio with real palms. You were served by a waiter in a white jacket and beer was fifty cents a bottle. I seem to have noticed a lot but actually I was oblivious. I was also so nervous I had to keep excusing myself rhythmically to go to the bique. Most human beings poop away their years waiting for some shimmering, mystic, way-far-out thing to happen, which is about as fruitful as peeling papayas. To most of them it never does. It just had to me. And I was in a condition of awe that bordered on the religious.

Incidently, I was already in love with him; desperately and spastically in love with him.

I didn't even know where Brown was geographically except it had to be somewhere around Cornell and Dartmouth but even that was irrelevant. When he had written that magic word in the sand it was as though a bell had been rung and I had begun to salivate.

Meanwhile I sat across from Ryder in bare feet and a sunburn trying to appear haute couture but actually in a Pavlovian panic. I had never felt so Carter City. I can't recall the conversation in detail or sequence but following are a few items.

His favorite sports were tennis and swimming but he intended to become serious about golf.

His father was vice-president of the bank in South Nuxton.

Brown University is located in Providence, Rhode Island.

His name was Ryder Smith.

He knew very little about the U except that it is a football powerhouse. He teased me by being surprised that we have classes and a faculty and stuff.

His home was in South Nuxton, Massachusetts.

He would graduate in June with a degree in General Business. He could not major in Specific Business because Brown was very fussy about turning out a well-rounded man, that is, one who, though he might major in a general area, would still have a liberal education, that is, a product characterized by breadth rather than depth.

His parents had shipped him to Europe for the Grand Tour last summer. There were two boys from Brown and two from Dartmouth and it had been a ball. The two incidents he could recall most vividly were a road race north of Naples on Lambretta motor scooters with some Wellesley girls which wound up in an Italian military cemetery and playing volleyball in the Colosseum. I must have looked blank.

"We were two days and three nights in Rome," he explained, "and the last night got very stoned on cognac. It's standard operating procedure to see the Colosseum by moonlight."

"Of course," I said.

"So that's where we wound up. Don't ask me where we got the volleyball. But it was practically the crack of dawn and no moon, so we climbed down to the floor of the place and got up a game. The floor of the arena isn't clear, you know, there are all those old A.D. pens where they used to keep the beasts."

"I know," I said.

"So we divided into teams, the Lions and the Martyrs. What an eerie game, you couldn't even see the other team, but the pen walls made a net and we zoomed the ball back and forth blind till we sobered up."

"Who won?"

"The Martyrs naturally." Ryder flashed a smile. "Providence was on our side."

My main contribution to this cosmopolitan chitchat was to describe how every few years a small boy hauled a large trout out of the Carter City millpond and had his photo in the papers.

We spent maybe an hour at The Sheikh's. I know all that Kipling jazz about Midwest is Midwest but the twain *had* met and I was about helpless with humility and love. These were some of my judgments of Ryder.

He was the costly gift in the simple package.

His sure movements, perfect manners, well-modulated tones, the repose and assurance of his expressions, were proof that he was human being bred in the best of taste.

He was the end-result of many generations of the best food, liquor and education.

He was the ultimate victory in the long process of social selection.

He was the triumph of the gene.

He was a gentleman.

"Would you care to see where I live?" he asked.
"I'd like that," I said.
Walking to his car I remarked how many police were roaring around on motorcycles.
"They increase the force this time every year," Ryder said. "Pull in some outside bulls."
"How come?"
"Otherwise the kids practically take over. Living it up is one thing but destroying property is something else."
The police seemed scarier to me than the kids. They were big red-faced beefeaters wearing crash helmets and khaki uniforms of some military sort and their motorcycles were Martian with antennae.
"Right?"
"What?"
"The destruction of property."
"I guess."
Walking with him I was glad to discover Ryder was at least two inches taller than I. My other discovery was a shocker. I had imagined his car would be no less than a Jaguar. It was a '55 Chevy two-door sedan, black. It was an adequate car and in very good condition but it was completely out of character. We got in and headed west, away from the ocean. I thought Fort Lauderdale consisted of Atlantic Boulevard and the beach, but Ryder said no, inland lived the real residents, those who wintered here. I gaped. After two or three bridges over canals which connected, he explained, with the Bahia-Mar Yacht Basin, which in turn connected with the channel to the ocean, he turned off on Chula Vista Drive. After another block he pulled into a semicircular driveway before a mansion of brilliant white stucco. There were royal palms and hibiscus and bougainvillaea and beds of roses. Ryder parked the Chevy in front of a three-car garage.
"You tell me," I said.
"I live here."
Using a key he let us in the door. I had never been in such a palace. I followed him around sort of like a flower in a crannied wall. A living room the length of a bowling alley, formal dining room fit for royalty, innumerable bedrooms with matching baths, all furnished fabulously, carpeted and air-conditioned. In the kitchen, an appliance heaven, Ryder took a tray of ice cubes from a pink refrigerator large enough to live in and led me onto a terrace replete with more palms and flowers and a colored gar-

dener crawling in and out of the shrubbery and a swimming pool. Beyond the terrace green lawns unrolled down a slope to a wide canal. Tied up to a dock was a long sleek white-and-mahogany yacht which I assumed was for quick Venetian trips to the supermarket. Across the stern was its name, in gilt: *Ataxia II*, Ft. Lauderdale.

"Shall we go aboard and have a drink?" Ryder said.

"I don't mind," I said boredly.

They say the legs go first and crossing the lawns mine nearly did. I am not *utterly* provincial. I have looked at lots of picture magazines and seen lots of movies and I knew the rich are rich but I had not realized *how*.

Ryder gave me the gracious, deluxe tour of the *Ataxia II*, from the flying bridge to the twin Diesels which powered it. A Chris-Craft, it slept ten and boasted a shower, three heads and a ship-to-shore telephone. I sat regally in the main salon while he made drinks. Most of the palaces along Chula Vista seemed to have their own yachts parked on the canal. The grandest boat I had ever been on was a fourteen-foot outboard with a dead fish on the floor.

"How much does a boat like this cost?"

"Roughly a thousand a foot. This is fifty-five feet."

"What happened to the depositors at your father's bank?"

"When?"

"When he took off with all the money?"

"This place isn't his, or the boat either. They're my uncle's. He and my aunt are in South America so they invited me to stay here. I'm sort of the prodigal nephew."

He went on to say that his parents were only comfortably fixed, as it were, while his uncle owned a small plant in South Nuxton which had prospered enormously during and since WW II. "He snagged a subcontract to make couplings for aircraft hydraulic systems. They were very good and Couplequip, that's the name of his company, has had practically a monopoly ever since. As a matter of fact, he's made so much money that the family thinks it's a bit gross. For example, this is a tax boat, Florida is full of them. You buy a boat, invite some of your sales people down in the winter, take them out for some fishing and call it a sales meeting. This makes the price of the boat and all the running expense tax-deductible. That's why he gave it the name, for laughs. He wants me to go in with him after graduation so I suppose the idea is that when he retires in a few years I'll take over."

"Are you going to?"
He brought the drinks. We raised them.
"To the U," he said.
"How come?"
"Because you go there. Because I've wanted to meet someone like you for a long time."
"To Brown," I said, touching rims. "Also cocoa, beige and taupe."
"Why?"
"Ditto."
Ryder stood there in his tanned, aristocratic wrapping and I sat there in my sunburn and oil and no lipstick and my hair a horror and we looked at each other in that tender-ravenous way we had on the beach only this time with both eyes.
"Merrit," he said, "will you sleep with me tonight?"
"Are you going to, Ryder?"
"What?"
"Go in with your uncle?"
"O, that. I have to decide. I have to consider what's best over the long haul. That's one reason why I came down here, to give it a lot of brain time. Well, will you?"
"Ryder, what kind of drink is this?"
"Gibson."
"I've never had one. What's in it?"
"It's like a martini except with an onion. Well?"
"Ryder, do you get good grades in school?"
"My God."
"I like to ask fundamental questions right away, like about grades and God and stuff. It gets you down to bedrock faster."
"So do I. Well?"
"But what about your grades?"
"No one goes after 'good' grades any more. That's collegiate. You go in for the 'right' grades. You plan from the first semester to commencement and the central point is, don't be conspicuous."
"Be a human zero?"
"No. Companies want an applicant to be intelligent but not too intelligent. If you are gung-ho and shoot for A's, that puts you in the grind category. Thanks to the damn Russians, the gentleman's C is out. So I've been trying for B's, and not just a B average, which gives you a margin for misses, but a flat, dependable B in every subject. It's very tough to pull off. For example, fall semester I had a

Poly Sci course I liked too well, so without meaning to I aced it. Even though that A brings up a C one joker handed me my sophomore year, it worries me. Looking over my transcript a personnel man may be convinced I'll be erratic politically, vote a split ticket, that kind of thing."

"Ryder, what was it you asked me?"

"I forget. O, will you sleep with me tonight?"

"Straight-arrow, why do you want me to?"

"I think it's the most sensible way to find out if we have love potential."

"I see."

"Well, Merrit?"

Love potential! With this succulent boy, this paragon, this ivy-wreathed god among American college men, when I had been mentally hurtling into bed with him every five minutes from the instant we met! Peering into the gin I tried telling my fortune. Could the daughter of a small-town druggist find happiness playing the role of Mrs. Ryder Smith? I had a fast montage of Balenciaga gowns, Moritz and Antibes in the winter, New York in the autumn, La Jolla and Newport in the summer, Givenchy frocks, Aiken in the spring, an apartment on Sutton Place South, a beach spread at Malibu, a lodge on a Scottish moor for bombarding grouse, a villa athwart Montego Bay, a wee hearth in South Nuxton, Massachusetts, with twenty-eight rooms and a brace of Bentleys rampant in the garage, etc. He would be my Fitz and I his Zelda and for a few rare years it would be mad, mad. Then at thirty the miracle: we would settle down, design a charming child or two and grow old together gracefully, patricianly and richly, courtesy of Couplequip. The onion, which in shape and color resembled at first a pith helmet, blurred, swelled, became a volleyball.

"I'd love to, Ryder," I said.

"Great," he said.

We finished our drinks in silence.

"What time shall I pick you up?"

I couldn't answer. I had no precedent. It was so different from making a movie on time or a dance or going somewhere for pizza.

He helped. "Would nine be all right?"

"Isn't that sort of avid?"

"Late to risc, carly to bed, makes a girl healthy, wealthy and *wed.*"

"Nine is fine," I said.

We left the boat and the house and he drove me home. There was no discussion. When he let me out at the Shalimar I was so tense and uncoördinated that when he put out his hand to take mine I shook it, which was so unfeminine that I blushed, I really did, which made the whole episode even more marshy.

No sooner did I walk into the apartment than I realized. He had not even kissed me. We had not even necked. Here I was signed up to consummate with a boy and we had not observed a single damn amenity! Now I may sound quite carnal from time to time but the fact is that I have had about as much experience at amour as I have at writing a book. I had made out; that is, made out in toto; with only one other boy besides TV Thompson, about which more later; yet I had just said yes to an approach so direct it would have been insulting if I had not already been in love with Ryder. Of course, its very directness made it even more metropolitan. In any event, the whole deal so shot me down that I draw a blank on what I did for the next four hours. I panicked. I took about six showers. I kept praying Tuggle would show up because she had so many battle stars and could give me the straight scoop on How To Prepare For An Assignation yet also praying she wouldn't because I would have to tell her the score. I redid my fingernails and toenails. I even tried some eye shadow for the first time; Tuggle had packed in plenty of supplies; but when I saw myself in the mirror I looked so much like a demimondaine or something that I burst into tears and smeared and had to make up all over. I forgot to eat but would have barfed if I had. There had been room in my suitcase for only two dressy dresses and I tried on each several times and finally flipped a coin to decide. For the last hour I sat biting my nails and thinking of smart remarks Abby Van Buren could make in her column about an operation like this and dying a slow moral death. Then a knock. A boy from the Big Ten would have summoned by horn but Ryder had come to my door and I loved him the more for it. I calmed and opened.

"Hi."

"Hi."

We smiled and he bowed low with his terrific eyelashes and we left the Shalimar with such aplomb we might have been off to a cotillion.

I assumed we would go to the castle on Chula Vista where we could sport around all fourteen rooms like amorous birds of prey plus aboard the yacht but instead Ryder piloted his Chevy north on Atlantic.

"Aren't we going to your uncle's?"

"Merrit, I've given it a lot of thought and decided against. Abuse of hospitality and so on." He shook his head. "No, he let me have the place to *live* in."

"Not to wench in, you mean," I said with a trace of bitters.

"It isn't that. As a matter of fact, I just feel using it for our purpose would be a bit uncricket."

I could understand his scruples since he was so obviously a gentleman but it did seem to me that if you were going to sin you might as well do it in luxurious surroundings. However, he drove north out of Lauderdale on the ocean highway almost to Pompano Beach and finally turned in at a motel and asked me to wait in the car while he registered. I waited. The motel has become the premarital proving ground of America and this one seemed more than usually Dantean and furtive. Finally I got out of the car to avoid feeling trapped. I was not afraid of being seen because it was sort of a John Milton Hilton, in other words, so dark you might as well have been blind. Squinting, I moved along the walk. Most of the cars had school stickers from states like New Jersey and Connecticut and Massachusetts from which I gathered this must be a favorite one-night pit of the Ivy League players. Out by the highway a neon sign winked lewdly and succinctly on and off: "MOTEL INNERSPRING MATTRESSES VACANCY." It might more aptly have read "Abandon hope all ye who shack up here." I was doomed. The shy scullery maid and the squire's lecherous son. I could vision us caught, surrounded by a morbid mob and reporters and police in crash helmets training submachine guns and searchlights on our room, ultimating us to come out hands-up or be gassed, both sets of parents summoned and bereavedly imploring us over loud-speakers to surrender, headlines, etc. I was ready to thumb my way back to Lauderdale when Ryder returned and ushered me through a door. He turned on a light, revealing a grubby little cubicle which was practically all bed. I mean this literally. So small was that room that the bed seemed as large as the flight deck of the carrier *U.S.S. Forrestal*. Ryder was locking and testing and retesting the door.

"Ryder," I said, "do you think the U.S. was wrong about the Aswan Dam?"

He lowered the window shade carefully.

"Ryder," I said, "does Brown have a good library?"

He eased off his beautiful pullover sweater.

"Ryder," I said, "what about inflation?"

He came toward me. I shrank. If he touched me I would scream. Instead, as soon as he took me in his arms I pelted him with tears.

"Merrit, darling," he said gently, "don't be afraid."

"I'm not afraid!" I sobbed. "And I'm not being coy but I've never done this before and unless you love me in some reasonable proportion to how much I love you I think this is just the *end*, the absolute *end*!"

"Darling, it may be the beginning," he protested. "At this stage love is irrelevant."

"It is?" I sniffed.

He said certainly, to come lie down with him and we would discuss it, but first he had better help me off with my dress so that we would not wrinkle it and I, practically palsied with love, allowed him to and then we were lying together and he was explaining how vastly times and mores had changed. For a girl to refuse a boy out of prudishness or fealty to some future husband and all that jazz was as archaic as a boy's trying to seduce a girl by means of liquor or brute force or what was once called a "line."

"Sex isn't a matter of morals any more," he assured me. "It's part of *personal relations*."

"It is?"

He kissed me and let me touch his eyelashes.

"Of course. It's the pleasant, friendly thing to do, Merrit, like shaking hands or making sure you catch the other person's name when you're introduced. We have to get along with people, there's nothing more important today. Saying no is antisocial. In what shape would we be if everyone went around rejecting each other?"

I had no answer because he turned my head and put his tongue tip in my ear, which no boy had ever done before. The sensation was absolutely classic.

"But what about love?" I whispered.

"Later, darling, later, after we're acquainted. Then if it happens it will be real and lasting because based on good personal relations, not on sex."

"O. O, Ryder," I shivered because he kissed me and turned me to him in a passionate yet poetic way that made me recall some lovely lines by A. E. Housman and we were so feverish and young and exciting together. "But what about virtue?"

"My God. Virtue can't be a physical thing, Merrit. It has to be spiritual. It isn't whether you have sex or not, it's your *attitude*."

His mouth was so sweet.

"If you make love purely for your own pleasure, it's probably wrong, but if you do it unselfishly, to please someone else, it's got to be virtuous."

We clave to each other and somehow his shirt and various other of our impedimenta had been removed.

"It's like contributing to charity, darling. Or working on a civic committee."

"Dear, dearest Ryder."

"As a matter of fact," he murmured fervently, "it's actually serving your fellow man."

Incidently, this was why I had decided in high school to become a teacher, to serve humanity, and why, at the U during fall term, I was dual-enrolled in Elementary Education and Core College. My courses were Core Lang, Core Sci, Core Liv, Basic Bowling; which was the only Phys Ed course I could get into because I registered the last day but was reputed to be convenient in case a coed married beneath her station, i.e., a noncollege man who did nurdy things like bowl; and two Ed courses, Principles of Piano and TPF. Principles of Piano was required so that the young teacher could accompany her pupils singing selections such as "America the Beautiful" and "Whole Lotta Lovin' " but since the U's budget had been axed by the state legislature there weren't enough pianos so we learned tunes on paper keyboards. It was sort of unknown, a whole classroom of girls sitting at cardboard Steinways not producing sound once though every week we could take five-minute turns at a real instrument. TPF stands for Theoretical and Practical Foundations of Elementary Education and was supposed to answer in one term for every girl this question: Do I *really* want to be a teacher? TPF was very Mickey Mouse. About a hundred girls sat in a lecture section day after day listening to pep talks about the needs of the nation's children, low pay on earth but high salaries in heaven, the quality of mercy is not strained, the patriotism of the American School Board, organize, summers off to travel abroad la-la-la, the red-hot status of the teacher in the community, bountiful retirement plans, money is the root of all evil, organize, the dignity and glory of the profession, the objectivity and altruism of the average P.T.A., the kicks you got out of molding young clay and kindling the light of learning in little eyes, and in general going out to fight-fight-fight for the future, etc., when almost every girl knew damn well what a royal goosing teachers take from society. Most of them majored in El Ed because, as I said earlier, it was the chic as well as the prudent thing to do; that is, you dated more and married sooner if boys found out you were getting a certificate and could bring home that second pay check after your childbirth chores were done. I was among the dedicated few. I fogged around campus having epiphanies about being the most Aztec teacher in history. That is, my one desire was to drape myself over the altar of an untutored world and let it cut out my heart. The climax of TPF was the half-day, late in the term, when each girl visited a live classroom in the local system. This was supposed to be her litmus test. She would observe the teacher in action and if she turned red with resolution she had a career. Out of the lottery I drew a second-grade room in a school close to campus and presented myself after lunch one blizzardy day in early December to a teacher whose name I have sublimated. Miss X introduced me to the kids; she had thirty-eight of them; and I had just nestled into a corner to observe when she was brought a message her mother, aged eighty-something, had fallen downstairs again because of her trick hip and Miss X had to go home. She and the principal voted to throw me into the breach as their substitute budget was skimpy and besides, all I had to do was amuse the darlings for two hours, which would be a snap. I was too shot down and challenged to protest. Miss X gave me last-minute instructions in the hall while putting on her hat.

"Now dear, they are mostly faculty children and so their parents are naturally experts on education but you will find them very advanced and precocious, O, my poor mother. Confidentially, many of them test in the genius range so the thing to remember is, *maintain control,* that's the sign of the *professional* teacher, and if one or two become troublesome here's a tiny trick." And with one hand she gripped me with such force where spine and shoulder meet that I almost passed out with pain. "There's a nerve or something there, dear, O, my poor mother, it's a dandy little device when you need it because there are regulations against spanking or slapping, so bye-bye, dear, and remember, *maintain control.*"

I took the field practically paralyzed. I will not attempt to be coherent about what transpired the next two hours. They looked at me and I looked at those thirty-eight precocious dimplers and absolute hell broke loose. Later I came to two conclusions. First, we have brought forth a generation of little monsters because the modern home is no longer a family group with discipline and stuff but a high-production *hatchery,* and second, there is no *teaching* time. We started with spelling and since they were all faculty children and geniuses I said we would dispense with kid words like cat and rat and I board-listed a bunch of words like gregarious and ethnocentrism and pedagogue and ordered them to memorize and then take a test when I felt something devouring the nylon about my left ankle; we had been told to wear hose and heels while observing; and I screamed and looked down and it was a damn *hamster,* I am serious, which completely flipped the class. They were allowed to have a room pet and this was it, a hamster, which they had y-clept Dido. We had a shout-down for a while during which two boys locked themselves in a death struggle for supremacy under a table and I was unable to separate them because I could not locate the nerve or something where necks and shoulders met. Then I trussed all thirty-eight of them into snowsuits and boots and we trooped out for recess into the blizzard and played kickball. It is great fun to race for first base in high heels and deep snow and get a kickball in the garterbelt. After that I blew noses and boys carted armloads of milk into the room for Milk Time, which was supposed to restore their eight-year-old energy after the rigors of learning, and while I was arbitrating who had paid for crackers and who hadn't as they wolfed down a whole box one of the boys came up with a loose front tooth which I pulled with pleasure, roots and all. We finally got going on ethnocentrism again when one of the girls cried, "Dido's coming all to pieces!" That damn hamster was having a *litter* right on the damn floor! After we had all assisted with the lying-in and Dido had blessed us with six or ten hairless dabs; the children said the father was the third grade's buck rabbit; I achieved a modicum of *control* by telling them the story of the Saint Valentine's Day gangster massacre in Chicago. Just as I was commencing to feel *professional* about seven girls went into convulsions while passing around a note which I snatched:

"I love you
I ador you

Pull down your pants
Let me xplore you."

I did not bother to locate the nerves of the two boys who proudly claimed authorship; I simply belted them in the jaw. There was much Florence Nightingaling among the girls and the other boys formed a flying wedge. According to the clock I had only fifteen minutes to go. On an inspiration I rushed to the record player and put on a march, "Columbia, The Gem of the Ocean," and grabbing the flag from its socket I began marching around the room. One by one they joined the parade and began to sing the words which they had somehow had time to learn, Lord knew how. With only eight minutes left we were merrily rattling the sabers when a woman entered and shouted to me she was the Room Mother and had come to ascertain if the teacher wanted her to serve cookies or cupcakes and Cokes or fruit punch for the birthday party next week and what about the Christmas Party and where was Miss X and if I was a substitute teacher this was a unique way to *maintain control* and she would report it immediately to the Superintendent and the National Education Association. It was the ultimate low blow. When we circumnavigated the room to her I yelled over the din that she could serve the little bastards *wood alcohol* for all I cared, I was only a coed observer trying to find out if I wanted to be a teacher and if she and her female pals were going to be so goddam *prolific* as to Mother every Room in America with thirty-eight mutations the least they could do was pay enough taxes so the system could afford substitutes and she could report me to the Supreme Soviet of the U.S.S.R. for all I cared but I wanted her to know the profession had just lost a damn good *pledge*. With that I jammed Old Glory into her hands and shoved her into the Grand Marshal's position and told *her* to take over and in hysterics cut the chaos. Incidently, I heard later from another coed observer that the first grade had a monkey.

That was the beginning of My War With American Higher Education and why I switched to Home Ec for winter term and eventually wound up in the Counseling Clinic with Dr. Edelson and his itchy feet.

"Are you sad I'm not a virgin?"

"No."

"You have a beautiful body, Ryder."

"Yours is great."

"Are you starting to love me slightly?"
"How can I help it?"
"Let's play another game."
"Game?"
"Volleyball."
"You darling."

I had to face a bitter fact: inexperienced though I was, having been up to bat with only three boys, counting Ryder, I was already cosmopolitan enough to recognize that there is a difference in the way they make love. A single swallow may not make a summer but it may tell you a lot about the martini as a genre. The word for Ryder was *efficient*. He attended carefully to detail; he left nothing to chance or inspiration. It was as though he had planned a B average in bed.

"Ryder, I wonder what I love most. You or what you stand for? I mean what you symbolize. Midwestern coeds have a vision of what Ivy League boys are like. That's why they come to Lauderdale."

"For example."

"Well, you're all mental giants, you had to be to be accepted, you're all beautiful and damned and scions to large old railroad fortunes. Between tutorial sessions you sit around studying at the feet of statues of people like Cotton Mather on green, storied campuses which are very conducive. *Esquire* photographers are always taking your pictures because you are such sharp dressers."

"Really?"

"Really. On week ends you play polo or foxhunt but mostly dash off in Jaguars and Alfa-Romeos to New York. There, under the clock at the Biltmore, you meet mink-lined Salinger-type heiresses who attend exclusive girls' schools and carry spare diaphragms and prayer wheels."

"Salinger-type?"

"He's a writer. Then you wind up the next dawn at mad, mad parties in Greenwich Village drinking with fascinating characters right out of Capote."

"What do we do after graduation?"

"Sit down and write yourselves up for *Who's Who in America.*"

"Is that all?"

"No, you live terrifically Fitzgerald lives."

"What's that?"

"Ryder, don't you read *anything?*"

"Merrit, my major is General Business."

"F. Scott Fitzgerald was a very fine writer who drank himself to death in Hollywood, which made him an even better writer. He went to Princeton."

"Naturally."

"Anyway, this is what you symbolize to romantic little coeds from the Midwest. Compared to you, Big Ten boys are cubes. Two years ago a girl at the U met a boy from Penn down here and they stayed right on after vacation was over and were married. It's been the biggest news in the girls' dorms ever since. That's why we come to Lauderdale with every gland going berserk." I kissed him because he looked so puzzled and content. "So what do you say, F. Scott?"

"I'll do my best to play the role."

I was holding Ryder in my arms when I began to hear a conversation going on in the room next to ours. There were two voices, a boy's and a girl's, and the girl's was Susy's! She was in bed with one of the three Yale boys! They must have been as close to the wall as we and as they talked Ryder and I resumed so that the only way I can convey the Sophoclean horror and coincidence of it all and keep it straight is to use dialogue.

SUSY

Do you really love me, Dilworth?

DILWORTH

You know it.

SUSY

I'd never have come here if you didn't. But I don't know who to believe. I mean, Jack and Pont say they love me, too.

ME

Ryder, you said you'd been wanting to meet a girl like me for a long time. Clue me.

DILWORTH

Be democratic, Suse. Believe all of us.

RYDER

I meant a coed from the Midwest.

SUSY

You're teasing. Dilworth, do you know why I love you mostly? Because you're from Yale.

ME

Why?

DILWORTH

Logical.

RYDER
O, at Brown we've heard a lot about them.
SUSY
No, it's more than that. I mean, you're romance and glamour and wealth and society and sophistication rolled into one. None of the boys at Michigan State can match that.
ME
For example.
DILWORTH
True.
RYDER
How warm you are.
SUSY
Last year a girl from State met a boy from Columbia down here and they got married. At least that's what I heard.
ME
You mean sexy.
DILWORTH
Those Columbia jokers are overintellectual. They act on impulse.
RYDER
No. Friendly, affectionate, coöperative. The perfect wife-mother-home type. And also that they're so sold on League men.
SUSY
Tell me honestly, Dilworth. Are Eastern girls different from Big Ten coeds?
ME
So easy to sheet in with.
DILWORTH
You know it. By sixteen they've been *used*. Then they get sort of cold and jaded. Great material for a matriarchy.
RYDER
I didn't say that, Merrit.
SUSY
What about us? Why do Leaguers like us?
ME
You implied it, though. The word is, we're all motel-happy, isn't it? And so you unzip and whip down to find out if it's true!
DILWORTH
You're more like European girls. Fresh, natural, pliant. You know how hot the troops are for European girls. They give the male his due. They never say *non*.

I sprang from the bed, snatched my things, darted into

the closet, slammed the door and there, with much clanking of hangers and nearly suffocating with shame and mortification, dressed myself and demanded of Ryder that he take me home immediately. When I emerged he was fully attired and we went directly to the car. The last sight I had of that dreadful Dade County Gomorrah was the neon sign, which was now winking "No Vacancy," and the hell there isn't, I thought.

It was an eternity from Pompano to Lauderdale. We did not speak. But at the Shalimar, when Ryder came around to open the door, I had regained enough self-respect to hope he was not furious, I still loved him tremendously, but if our relationship were to ripen it would have to be on a nonsexual basis. He assured me he understood my sensations, he admired, even loved me for them, and he was so darling and Spartan about it that I kissed him and made a date for the next day.

To my apprehension, Tuggle was not home and it was after midnight. I put on pj's and waited for her. I felt abysmal and slutty. Once again I had gone without dinner and was so undernourished that while waiting I lost three falls out of three to my conscience, especially when I caught a vision of poor, thin, betrayed Herbert TV Thompson making a lonely safari in his pith helmet up and down the beach all afternoon and half the night searching for me. And less than twenty-four hours ago I had said I could love him! Around one o'clock Tuggle showed.

"Where were you, Tug?"

"Date."

"Nice time?"

"Keen. Where were you?"

"Date."

"Nice time?"

"Keen."

"Who with?"

"Boy from Brown."

"Brown?"

"Providence, Rhode Island."

"The League?"

"From the founding."

"Where'd you go?"

"Hither and yon."

I clapped a hand over my mouth to stifle a scream. She was wearing her swim suit and carrying a bag of potato chips!

"TV!"
"So?"
"You dated TV!"
"You weren't around, I was. So don't bark at me from the manger," she said defiantly. "He's very sweet and I've never been so sorry for a boy. Do you know what happened to him at school? He's never told anybody but he had a date with a sorority queen . . ."
"You fell!" I cried. "That's how he got his name and all he needs is a nice girl to love him and you fell the way I did and Barbara Hutton did and we're not even immoral any more, Tug, we're *promiscuous!*"
We collapsed. We wept. She told me how beautiful it had been by the yacht basin in the moonlight and how she had cracked her vow of chastity not once but twice with that subtle of subtles, TV, and we wept about that.
"I'm the whore of the college world!" she wailed.
"No, I am!" I wailed.
I told her about Ryder and his mansion and his yacht and the motel and little Susy being seduced in the next room and we wept about that. Perhaps it is time to confess that the biggest problem any girl brings to Lauderdale is not really Life but Man.
"We're not solving anything or going anywhere or even having fun!" I bawled, my mouth full of potato chips. "We're having a sexathon!"
"It's the tropics!" Tuggle boo-hooed. "You simply go to hell in the tropics!"
Incidently, Tuggle is her last name but her first, Barbara, none of her friends uses because it sounds like some heroine leaning from the tower of some Sir Walter Scott castle.

4

Most of the recent studies of courtship in America consider random dating as real courtship—that is, as a learning experience which eventually leads to marriage. Emotional self-control is most essential in random dating. It is like a poker game. Deep emotion is inappropriate.

INTERPERSONAL RELATIONSHIPS

Mass migration from the north was about ended although a few kids continued to make colorful entrances. For example, an entire fraternity of engineers from Purdue had pulled into Lauderdale the day before riding in five ancient black hearses with sirens shrieking and announced themselves by a parade down Atlantic Boulevard which blocked traffic and had to be broken up by the police. For another, the same day, a fourteen-man choral group or glee club from Princeton which called itself The Nassoons arrived in a sort of derelict schooner from a week's singing and drinking tour of the Bahamas and was put ashore in a dinghy and immediately gave a concert of such rousing Princeton airs as "The Orange and The Black" and "New Jersee" for the youthful multitudes on the beach. But the most spectacular arrival was staged the next day, by accident. Tuggle and I were seeking solace from the sun after the bitter revelations of the night before. We had sworn off sex for the duration and sealed the pledge in tan oil. First Ryder happened along and I introduced him to Tuggle, which was okay, but second TV appeared and Tuggle and I would have ignored him except that it is difficult to slough off anyone wearing a huge hat of palm fronds or something with "I'll Remember Nassau!" in large corny letters so I had to introduce him to Ryder and then the four of us stood around for several taut minutes wondering who was thinking what about who.

"Great weather, hey?" Tuggle said.

"Great," we all said.

Pause, while at least three of us began to sense the horror implicit in incest.

"Does anyone have any ideas about NATO?" I suggested.

Pause, while they stared as though I had gone stark.

"I'll remember Nassau," Tuggle said.

It was Jackson, The City of Action, who saved the scene. "How about," he said, his hands birding, "how about the four of us doubling tonight and taking in some of the plush places?"

"Great," we all said as though it was.

But the motion passed and the meeting was adjourned with relief. After the boys had gone and Tuggle was remarking how darling Ryder was, those brown orbs and things, and she did not blame me for last night's picnic on Venus the hiatus was shattered by an earsplitting scream of brakes followed by an explosion. A row of parking spaces separates the beach from the Boulevard. Into one of these spaces had careened a car at such high speed that it had overshot the curb, blown a tire, and trumpeting its horn and scattering kids in all directions finally lurched to a stop in the sand. Everyone ran up to see. It was a real apparition. The car was a gigantic, new Lincoln Continental Mark XX or something sedan with much mud and Ohio plates. One of its front fenders had been completely sheared off at an earlier date so that the engine and wheel and suspension were nakedly, almost obscenely exposed. Atop the car was a rack heaped not with luggage but with a minor mountain of what appeared to be cased musical instruments, among them recognizable the outlines of a string bass and a set of drums. On both sides of the Mark XX was this legend, in big gold: THE BASIL DEMETOMOS QUARTET: DIALECTIC JAZZ. Out of the car sagged four boys, the quartet obviously, not to assess the damage but to stretch and strip off their shirts and bare themselves to the sun. One of them was the hairiest boy I had ever been repelled by; his arms, chest, shoulders and even back were thicker than the jungles of Belgian Equatorial Africa. He was older than the others, though. Kids milled around the car and someone said the combo had driven straight through from Ohio State. A squad of boys pushed the Mark XX back up the beach and over the curb into the parking space and then there was a lot of laughing and talking and unloading of instruments from the rack and someone passed the word in return for the help the combo was going to play over at the Sheikh's. For kicks Tuggle and I went along with the crowd.

It was early afternoon so there was ample room in The Sheikh's for the combo to uncase and set up and audience to assemble. They were very nonchalant and built the suspense well. No one had the faintest idea what the sound would be.

Well, class, let me establish one thing in advance. I do not belong to the *cult;* in other words, I do not go ape over jazz. I don't know much about it and do not intend to specialize; if it is an art it is a minor art; besides, the national bushes are already overloaded with pretenders and *aficionados* who sit around with their heads in hi-fi speakers and make a great, metaphysical obsession of it. As you realize by now, when anything becomes a big deal I rebel out. This also goes for esoterica. I do rather care for several bands and singers and buy a record now and then but that is the extent of my development. If this makes me a stump, tough. Nor am I trying to play it cool. I abhor the whole concept of *cool,* in jazz or human endeavor or anything. If man had not burned for a few things he would still be grunting about in *cool* caves. *Casual* is okay, though.

The hairy one turned out to be the leader. At last he rapped for quiet and made the following announcement:

"This is it. Let me introduce Quent on piano, Archie on tenor, Ray on drums, and myself, Basil, on bass. This is a workshop, not a session. Why you fly you do not thank the Icarytic laws so no applause, please, as we wish the atmosphere to be as unfrantic and cerebral as possible. If you have questions, state them during the breaks. The first thing we'll do is an original titled 'Keep Britain Tidy.' And by the way, there will be free beer for all on The Quartet."

A cheer went up. The Basil Demetomos Quartet came down the chute. Everyone in The Sheikh's understood immediately that this was a nonjesting, professional group, with arrangements and everything. But with their first number began one of the oddest afternoons Lauderdale had ever known; I say afternoon because Tuggle and I left after about four hours. What happened was that we became involved. Each number was at least ten minutes and was followed by a break during which they would circulate and during the first one the pianist, a real weirdo, came over to talk to Tuggle. He seemed to be attracted to her the way a bullfrog is attracted by a flashlight. The drummer and tenor man were clean-cut college boys chewing gum, although with their shirts off; but bare to the waist that was exactly what Quentin resembled, a gigantic bullfrog on its two long thin legs. From the hips up he must have weighed two hundred pounds, below them no more than fifty. He had a white sleepy face, heavy neck and slope shoulders. The lenses of his horn-rims were so thick that behind them his eyes were as drab and beat-on as little snare drums. Tuggle, who was quite intrigued, asked him many questions but he was very difficult to talk to. They had driven from Columbus, Ohio, without a stop except for food and gas and Basil would not even let them turn on the car radio. He never permitted them to buy or play records. To most questions Quent would just smile a slow-burning smile at Tuggle and say, as though it were a communiqué of international significance:

"We are current."

Once he twined her hands with his tapering fingers and

said, like a child who has decided late in childhood to believe in the Easter bunny, "We could be prospective."

The next number was "Un Poco Loco," a standard.

Quentin brought Basil Demetomos back to our table with him.

"You are a big girl," he said to me. "Handsome, but very big."

This naturally delighted me. "What is dialectic jazz?" I asked. "I don't dig the dialectic."

He slammed down in a chair and flexed a bicep. He was very muscle-bound. "Among my hates are college students, political parties, television, fraternities, my century, status-symbol cars, my generation, advertising, groupism, and all military, social and religious organizations. But the highest priority I give to people who try to use jazz jargon. If you want to talk to me, keep it civilian."

His brutality confused me. "I don't understand about dialectic."

"And someone takes tuition from you. You should know the Socratic method of argument and investigation, question-and-answer. My conception of jazz is that it should be approached dialectically, that is, as a kind of search in which the music, its line and chord-structure, asks the most basic questions of the musician, and he, in attempting to answer them, supplies the fullest answers of which he is capable at any given moment. The result being that you have discovery on two levels, within the music and, equally important, within the musician. Jazz, then, should be a dialectic, or method. Provided it is valid. And provided you have the remotest glimmering in your coed mind what the hell I am talking about."

"I was going to compliment you," I remarked, "until you turned out to be a complete yo-yo."

I might have said worse, that with his bullet head and nose like a big thumb pushed into his face he was utterly repulsive but he was already leaving. He was also bow-legged.

"Our next number," he announced, "is an original of mine titled 'Nuclear Love Song.' "

To watch him play and sing at the same time was really odd. He was so short, not more than five-six, and sort of simian, that the string bass towered above him and he had to reach over his head and sing in a high-pitched, strainy voice, his Adam's apple as animated as a Mousecartoon, and clutch his bass close to him, nestling it into all that hair; and the total effect was quite interesting. He had been inspired to write this, he said, by reading recently in the papers that government scientists would soon announce a "safe" radiation exposure standard for the U.S. population. This would be about ten roentgens per person up to age thirty from all sources, including nuclear tests. Radiation records for everybody would determine what couples could safely be allowed to marry and reproduce. This was "Nuclear Love Song," which he sang to the tune and tempo of a lilting, happy waltz:

"In these times of international tensions,
Marriage may have mutational dimensions;
It's no longer enough to be morally pure,
A boy and girl have got to be genetically sure.
So although the subject seems somewhat macabre,
Before friends shower us with silver candelabra—

Baby, let's add up our roentgens
To see if we may love;
They're science's latest inventions,
More crucial than moonlight above.

Baby, let's add up our roentgens
To see if we may mate;
No matter how chaste our intentions,
We will probably procreate.

Radiation's okay in permissible amounts;
It's not the fall-in but the fall-out that counts!

So baby, let's add up our roentgens
To AEC if we may wed;
Though we love till we die—
If our count is too high—
Our children are already dead!"

"I retract everything," he said, returning to our table. "I am often called The Gloomy Greek. Compliment me."

"Okay," I said, sipping beer on The Quartet. "I like your song."

"The song? A bagatelle." From a plastic tube he drew a fat Havana Cordura or something cigar, gnawed off the end and lit it, puffing furiously. "I *do* play bass well. My upper register work is as irreproachable as that of any man in the country. In the lower Leroy Vinnegar's is much more agile but his left arm is longer."

The next number was another original titled "Cool in the Cotswolds."

Tuggle and Quentin resumed their mute dialogue. I heard him say once again that they could be now and she nodded as though she knew when that was.

"The combo," said Basil Demetomos, blowing cigar smoke as though our conversation had been uninterrupted, "is not yet good because it is derivative." That was why he did not allow the flock to listen, under any circumstances, to records. Archie, his tenor man, was still Gerry Mulligan to the core while Ray, his drummer, aped Mel Roach and since the child is father to the man he had forbidden auding anything until, purified at last, freed, they could all four break out into their original own, onto a new soundplane, at which point they could be truly valid. This, he estimated, might require another year. Until then he would keep the flock to its task, give them an occasional change of scene such as Florida, and minister to their inner harmony when needed. In the interim, while they waited on the laggards, Quentin could arrange and he, himself, could compose.

The next number was another standard, "Love for Sale."

The most mystic thing about The Quartet was that it was so *paradoxical*. For example, they would stop right in the middle of a number to repeat certain phrases or argue among themselves about the arrangement. About the audience they did not seem to give a damn. But on the other hand, every few minutes the waiters served beers to more than a hundred kids, which, at fifty cents per bottle, totted up to fifty dollars per round. This had to be the first musical outfit in history to pay people to listen; ridiculous in itself since they were good enough to charge admission; and then treat them with the disdain of scientists experimenting in some kind of lab.

"Why the bought audience?"

"To be disobligated. For the same reason that when we job in Columbus we never accept remuneration."

"You play for free?"

"I do. The flock I pay out of my own pocket. I take care of their school and living expenses and give them a small life-situation salary."

"Gads, why?"

The next number was an original titled "An Encounter between Coleridge and Carlyle on Hampstead Heath."

"To keep them uncorrupt," Basil Demetomos went on. "So that we don't have to play what and how people want. In that way we can learn together without tension."

"But this must cost scads."

He gripped the cigar as he might have a bone. "Big girl, I am also known as The Playboy Without Joy."

He announced another original of his, called "Saint Simon Stylites," and when they socked off the tee I caught on for the first time with ear and mind to the dialectic method. Throughout the piece, which was fast and hard-driving, Basil bowed a single high note, which had to be Stylites atop the pillar; but the search was carried on by tenor and piano alternating questions and answers, provoking each other to improvisation that went way far out abstruse. Getting their message, I began to bang with both bare feet. Of course my insights might have been thanks to Budweiser. I was so unaware of jazz I scarcely knew Brubeck from Sun Yat-sen. The Sheikh's was really in a sweat by now, kids standing up and weaving in appreciation. Tuggle and I compared notes. She had managed to mute more information out of Quentin, not about himself but about The Gloomy Greek. He was classified as a "special student" at Ohio State because he refused to major in anything, preferring to choose courses out of the catalogue as though it was a menu and education a banquet for the intellect; his grades were very high, the Lincoln Mark XX belonged to him, he camped out in a suite at the Deshler Hilton Hotel, the finest in Columbus, wined and dined lavishly, but had sworn the flock to celibacy and a stoic existence.

"Look at these kids," Basil said, gesturing with a fist around The Sheikh's, "having a ball. In a few days they will leave Lauderdale and go out into the world and ulcerate themselves like galley slaves, the boys oaring and the girls cracking whips of flannel over them, and for what? So that in twenty or thirty years they can all afford to come back to Lauderdale to have less delight than they have now."

Quentin, who had been carrying on a brisk pantomime with Tuggle, opened his mouth to speak to her.

"You have much outreach."

"Where did you get that word?" I cried. "What's the definition?"

He clung to Tuggle's hand. "I was erst."

I appealed to Basil Demetomos. "Can't you make him say? That word means a lot to me."

"I wouldn't if I could. Quent is an inverse Bud Powell case. Instead of being withdrawn, he is *emergent*. When he plays he withdraws *to* reality."

"What is this vocabulary of his? Current and prospective and stuff?"

"Unlike most musicians he's sensitive to time, not space. He fears the past and dreads the future. In the present he studies at the Happy Conservatory." He tapped Quent on the forehead. "Break's over, boy, back to *la belle dame sans merci.*"

The Quartet reassembled to do another standard, "Idaho."

During the next break I asked Basil about his Anglophilia as reflected in such titles as "Keep Britain Tidy" and in order to explain he had to brief me on his life situation. His father, Niklos, had journeyed alone to the U.S. at twenty-five, leaving his bride in Greece, and after lengthy employment as a waiter finally bought a small restaurant near the railroad station in Toledo, Ohio. When he was thirty-two, operating on a timetable known only to himself, he sent for his older brother Constantine to help him with the Peloponnesus Café. Meanwhile Basil had not yet been born because his mother-to-be was still awaiting her summons from the Old Country. It came in her fortieth year; she reached Toledo, produced Basil on schedule, and died of the effort, her function fulfilled. Basil grew to young manhood on a diet of roast beef, mashed potatoes and soot, the specialties, respectively, of the Peloponnesus Café and the B & O Railroad, living with his father and bachelor Uncle Con in dingy rooms over the restaurant. In lieu of baseball and cars and girls he was allowed to own and play a bass viol. After graduation from high school he enlisted in the Air Force, which branch of service shipped him o'er the wine dark sea to England. It was to be his odyssey. For two years he adventured not behind a tiller or before a radarscope or through a gunner's turret but from a librarian's desk at an interceptor base near Oxford. Life, he discovered, could be like Helen, a woman of legendary beauty, of infinite charm and wonder. He paid her passionate court. The youth whose only river had been the turgid Maumee now strolled the mossy banks of the Isis, the Cam, the Thames. He climbed the creaky wooden steps of the Bodleian to read. Backed by differing combos of brother airmen he flew at an extreme altitude and there found jazz. Toward the end of his enlistment Niklos died. Basil returned home and enrolled at Ohio State. He was twenty-three and a junior.

The next number was "My Funny Valentine."

Stammering his concern about the beer bill and the ability of The Quartet to pay it, the manager of The Sheikh's came to our table. He said it now stood at over $300. Basil Demetomos brought forth a roll of currency and dealt off five hundred-dollar bills.

"Let there be no dearth of mirth," said The Playboy Without Joy, returning the roll to his pocket.

Tuggle and I sat in a sort of stupor.

"America," he muttered. "Last year I wanted to treat the flock to a fine party so I ordered a barrel of oysters shipped from Baltimore. Then I worried, wouldn't they be dead of famine before they reached the party? I asked the man and he said no, they live off each other in transit. In the blackness of the barrel they open up and feed on the little marine flugs and nerrs that cling to their shells. That's America."

He rubbed his unshaven chin with disgust. I saw that there was premature gray at his temples. Outside The Sheikh's it was dusking and inside Bacchus reigned so supreme that my head throbbed with a dialectic beat. He was a fine one to talk about materialism after flashing a fortune, particularly without giving a clue how he had come by it. I did get the scoop subsequently, about which more later, but for the present I began to anger at his conceit and melodramatics. He looked around at the weavy kids.

"They like our sound."

"They like your beer."

"Tell your friend to unhand Quent."

"You don't own him."

"I've paid for him."

"You live as you please."

"I'm older."

"Jazz is a minor art."

"Will you tell me how the good goddam any man in this century deserves a *major* art?"

"Guano."

"Coed."

"Misanthrope."

He seized my knee savagely under the table.

"Big girl, date me."
"Let go."
"Date me."
"Or I'll kick you."
"I'll take you into the alley and beat you."
"Greek beast."
"Date me."
"I'd barf."
"Why?"
"I dislike you intensely."
"Impossible."
"Boor."
"But valid."
"Poseur."
"But rich."
"Hairy."
"Date me."
"Damn you, all right."
"Tomorrow night."

He let go of me and taking Quentin swaggered back to play. Tuggle and I were so limp from the afternoon and the impact of The Quartet we could scarcely plow out of The Sheikh's but we had dates.

The last sight I had was of the flock tearing off another original titled "Euston Station," torsos glistening with sweat, tenor and piano asking questions and giving answers, while in their midst, like a muscular rock, stood Basil Demetomos, his head wreathed in smoke from a fresh cigar. I did not know what I had assented to. So monkeylike was he that I would have bet money he had a bright red behind.

In one of the assigned readings for Core Living, which as I said before is a general education course all freshmen at the U have to take so they can learn early to live effectively, I ran across this list. Some prof took a survey on some campus to see what college students' biggest problems are. As I recall, here are the ones mentioned most often: 1. How to be popular. 2. How to improve our looks. 3. How to get the most out of our education. 4. What about sex? 5. How to be sure what profession you'll be happiest in. 6. How do I find out what I add up to? He was very bitter because they weren't world-wide in scope like white slavery or pill contraceptives or What Position Should The U.S. Adopt Re The Dispute Between India And Pakistan Over The Partition Of Kashmir, etc. That is one of the unfortunate characteristics of profs: they were never young. They forget, too, that students have the hell so surveyed out of them that they have become slick at evasive action. This doesn't mean that kids aren't *searchers;* they are. O, they refuse to scout around on the stage with the lights on in full view of the audience but later they slip in a side door when the house is dark and deserted and rehearse their part in the play in private. I am going round and round but my real point is this, that the above list of problems is picky and can be boiled down to four things: Wisdom, Love, Goal, Faith. Also, that society is no damn help. In fact, today it's a *drag*. Take Wisdom, for example. You have to acquire knowledge before you can be wise so the country has colleges and U's on which it spends almost as much as on cosmetics and gladly packs us off every autumn la-la-la, but then kids find the data they glean is supposed to be done undercover, without any trace of effort, including underarm. Be seen at the books too much or in the library too frequently and you are out of it, even with parents, who want you, above all else, to poop around with people. We want Love, but the world makes it so hard to define. In movies and TV and stories and other media it takes a mystic and wonderful form. But practically from puberty on we are warned in columns and marriage courses and by the omnipotent adult that passion is fleeting, soon fades the rose, so don't trust our emotions or found a marriage on them because what we think is romance is really base, animal instinct. Thus they take every kick out of Love, so that instead of the greatest it's the weediest thing that can occur to you. As to a Goal, all kids need one dementedly; but again, if they throw themselves into something like a club or profession or field they are being gung-ho rather than all-round, which is a sign of immaturity. Goal is certainly nothing they can mention in public. Besides, there's no need to save society any more; it's in swell shape. Finally, there is Faith. You believe yet don't believe. You are fairly convinced in your bones there is some Lifetime Friend who sort of *produces the show*, if you know what I mean, and who will check on you daily if you are decent. But believing in the Creation and Universal Sin and stuff like that is considered snapping your cap. Attend church, but not *habitually*. Believe, but don't make a *project* of it. Try *praying*, and they will take you away. And if you ever do lose whatever Faith you hung onto, don't worry about being agnostic or anything.

People will no more dare to inquire about the state of your soul than they will about your bowel movements.

Sometimes I am ticked off and unhappy but other times I remember that today there's a free coupon in every box. Society will provide. Give good old society enough time and it will pass out these things as liberally as scholarships or spending money or cars. You may have to wait in line a little but stick around and there'll be a campus for Love, about a million courses to choose from for Wisdom; none of them too tough; ample job opportunities for a Goal, and for Faith, lots of churches and activities. Everything is working for you. All that's actually removed from life is the *risk*.

The world is a great big dormitory in which we pay our fees to live for a few terms. We are placed three to a room designed for two. It may seem crowded but remember, that way we pay off the mortgage faster. I'm not sure that this is relevant right here but it's a swell analogy.

Congress should pass a law requiring every boy to dress as suavely for a date as Ryder. In his black summer suit and white button-down and small-patterned gray tie he was a dream of League understatement. I don't mean to imply anything derogatory about TV, either, because his light cord suit probably cost more than Ryder's and with his bones mercifully covered he looked tall and sharp. It was just that his white bucks were too new and his tie had sort of orange stripes and you expected it might light up any minute and read "Kiss Me, Baby!"

Tuggle and I were so glad to be going night-clubbing at last that we were ready when the boys came. We went in Ryder's car since TV's was only a two-seater. I'll skip very much about the early evening because the big news came later. We drank beer in a place called Via Condotti so dark you had to grope for your glass. Then we put in an hour at a very drunken, corny club I do not even know the name of which was a mob scene of fat tourists dancing like bears with each other's wives and palming their girdles. It had a one-man band, a guy who played piano and attached harmonica and sang into a mike the latest tunes such as "My Gal Sal." I remembered Basil Demetomos saying we'd all kill ourselves to return to Lauderdale in twenty years for this. I clue you, nobody can be more *fungous* than middle-agers on the grape.

Finally, though, we went to one of the swankest hotels, the San Remo, which featured a club called the Full Fathom Deep, and this was really unique. The keeno things were that it was under the hotel and beside the swimming pool and had large windows so that you could see subsurface into the blue, floodlit water. A lot of elegant clientele; minky, bored-type women and well-dressed men with bedroom tans; were listening and dancing to the strains of a three-piece combo. To discourage the peasants, beer was a dollar per bottle so we switched to mixed drinks and I had my first frozen daiquiri. Gads, it was classic!

Logically, the subject of money came up and I raved about Ryder's uncle's mansion and yacht and Couplequip and everything and it was at this point I got the strange and oriental story of Basil Demetomos' wealth. Tuggle told us. She had couched it from Quentin, as it were. Basil's only charge in boyhood, you recall, was playing the bass viol. His father's and Uncle Con's recreation had been reading *The Wall Street Journal*. Their dingy rooms were stacked to the ceilings with twenty years' accumulation of copies. When, after Niklos' death, Basil returned to Toledo he was informed his loving father had left him a fortune, after taxes, of $100,000, all of it in common stock in which the restaurateur had secretly been investing since the early 1930's, practically a penny at a time. He also inherited the Peloponnesus Café. This was all Tuggle knew.

Ryder danced impeccably.

"Do you approve of Tuggle, darling? She's my best friend."

"Great party girl."

"Isn't TV a character?"

"Very colorful."

"Don't you like him?"

"It isn't that. As a matter of fact, he's probably adequate as a person. But men from the Big Ten are so hardnosed around anyone from the League. I've noticed it before. They have a kind of built-in inferiority complex. Maybe it comes with their subscription to *Playboy* magazine. Not that I blame them, but it makes socializing rough."

He held me so close my daiquiri unfroze. Being there with him that way was absolutely empyrean.

"I wonder what all the dear poor people are doing tonight."

"Where?"

"Back in Carter City. I wish they could all be here for an hour. So they could have it, too."

"They should see you. You look great."
"Mmmmmmmmm."
"You weren't serious, were you?"
"When?"
"About our entering a no-sex era?"
"I have to be."
"Why?"
"Because I've waited so long to be in love. I really have, Ryder. I didn't even go through the usual infatuata in high school. I held back, waiting for the giant emotional jackpot. I'm scared about love in Lauderdale being vacationary. You know, just part of the trip, like a tan that turns to white. In other words, sweet, I want the real fiftieth-anniversary thing, not just bed now and pay later."
"But sex is part of love, Mer."
"Passion obsolesces."
"Where did you hear that?"
"In a marriage course."
"My God. Won't you relent?"
"I don't know."
"I do love you, Mer."
"Mmmmmmmmm."
When we were back with TV and Tuggle the very thing Ryder had mentioned reared its prejudiced head. The four of us fell to talking about schools and hostilities, fortunately oral, broke out between the boys. They went round and round about the relative merits.
"It's possible to get just as sound an education at a Midwest school," TV insisted. "It depends on the individual."
"But not probable," Ryder said. "You simply don't have the traditions."
"You mean you happened to be more contiguous to the Puritans. That's not necessarily bingo."
"Or the faculties. You have to beg funds from a gang of illiterate state legislatures. We're endowed."
"Yes, with loot your old grads screwed out of the Midwest in the first place!"
Ryder stayed very aloof but I was surprised by how bitter and William Jennings Bryanesque was TV. His hands shot over his cord suit searching for thread ends to pull and I expected him any minute to launch into a "Cross of Ivy" speech. It was the eternal conflict, I supposed, between the frontiersman and the entrenched Easterner. Hauling at his orange tie he demanded Ryder give his picture of the average Midwest school. Ryder said he was no

authority, he had never been west of Pittsburgh, travel by stagecoach was tiring and then of course there was the Indian problem, but the word he had was that our schools tried to be all things to all taxpayers and wound up in ineffectuality. They were giant brain-bakeries turning out identical loaves by means of IBM ovens. And that the hottest intellectual issues on their campuses were the allocation of football tickets and the condition of student parking lots. Finally, that the men graduated with only one aim in life.

TV ground an ice cube to bits between his teeth. "What?"

Ryder smiled. "To join the Diners' Club."

Herbert Thompson tipped over his chair, rose to his thin six feet four, and ran a hand through his crew-cut as though it were a coonskin cap. But I was on my feet beside him.

"Shall we dance?"

Before there could be blows I had him on the floor. He fairly trembled with boyish, regional rage.

"Traitoress!" he hissed.

"Adulterer!" I hissed right back.

It took the fight out of him and started his large feet moving so that we could at least go through dance motions. "You're a crook, TV," I said, "an amoral conman. I'm going to paint a scarlet A on your Porsche. And if it had been anyone else but Tuggle I'd never forgive you." He was so red-faced and such a disjointed dancer that I found him pitiable. "But she's my best friend and thinks you're sweet so for her sake I do."

He alibied that he had turned over practically every grain of sand on the beach looking for me before asking Tuggle for a date. "And I was serious about loving you," he protested. "I get so damn lonely, Merrit, and I have the obsession I have to locate someone, a girl, or something, a cause, to protect me against myself. Do you really like this effete guy?"

"We are in love," I said simply.

He held me at arm's length. "But two nights ago you said you could love me and maybe you did! So who, Hester Prynne, is tricky?" he demanded, shaking me slightly. "The Lauderdale Tondelayo!"

It was my turn to blush. Because it was true, I had made one semi and one absolute profession to two different boys in as many days, and what really compounded my confusion was that I had agreed that very afternoon to date a third, Basil Demetomos. That had been under physical duress, of course, but perhaps I *was* becoming the Becky Sharp of East Swander Dorm. I crept close to my accuser and we shuffled in silence.

"O, TV, I'm so embarrassed and sorry and shot down," I whispered at last.

"So am I."

"I did mean it by the yacht basin. But now I'm in love with Ryder. And I bet you told Tuggle you love her, too."

"I did."

"Whatever is happening to us?"

"Maybe we don't get enough to eat."

"Maybe."

To get us both off the hook I eventually said I'd been thinking about his future, commanding communication and stuff, but wasn't there a small matter he had overlooked? What about the service? It was a lucky topic because he also had plans for that. He was going into the Army after graduation and unionize it.

He pushed his shell-rims high on his forehead. "Who is the esne of history, the serf of every society? Who gets the lowest pay and longest hours and lousiest working conditions? Whose job is the most dangerous? The soldier! I tell you the service is a damn sweatshop, and unfair, unfair!"

We practically had to stop dancing because TV's hands took off in excitement and vision.

"So I'm going to organize the Army and after that the Air Force and Navy. It's time the youth of the country quit taking a royal raping every damn generation and got together, rank and file, and struck for a dying wage."

"How much?"

He pulled down his shell-rims. "What price survival, babyroo? In the clinch the soldier's function is more important than anybody else's, actually, so he should pull down as much as any executive or movie star or TV personality or political doddy who sits around signing stuff. I figure a half-million a year per man, with plenty of tax loopholes, and that's what we'll walk out for and stay out till we get."

"They'd put you in jail."

"The whole Army?"

"The country can't afford that much."

"Can't afford to save its neck? It has to! Maybe then it

won't be so damn offhand about drafting young men and putting on wars because they'll be expensive. Listen, Merrit, you hit this country in its standard of living and you win, pledge. Why not a soldiers' union? Everybody else has one. This the age of togetherness. And when we're solid over here we'll go international! Don't tell me our British and French and German and Chinese and Russian locals won't take to the picket lines for a half-million a year!"

The music ended and we had to return to our table because the lights in the Full Fathom Deep dimmed and a man came to a mike and announced their famous underwater floor show would now begin. He said to watch the pool and we would any minute meet Ramona, The Scylla of Sex, who had cast a spell over many a modern mariner and lured him to a delightful doom. Everyone waited, eyes fixed on the windows into the pool. Suddenly, with an explosion of bubbles, splitting the opacity of the water, she appeared. There were many ooh's and ah's from the assembled drinkers. She swam to the windows and began her act. Ramona had long *pink* hair, I am serious, *pink*. She wore a skin-tight gold swim suit and gold high-heeled pumps and about as gorgeous a figure as it is natural to have, long white legs and long white arms with many golden bracelets about her wrists. Her act consisted of graceful and suggestive gyrations in rhythm to the music from the combo which of course she could not hear, with also what seemed to be a few grinds. She must have had terrific lungs because only about once every three minutes did she glide to the side of the pool and take in air from a small rubber hose. Her climax was reaching for a bottle of Pepsi-Cola as it sank nearby, tilting it, and drinking the entire contents without inhaling or shipping water. She smiled and blew bubbles and bowed to much applause. It was really a unique routine and she was about to exit upward when it happened.

Well, class, I must interrupt here. I know this is really giving the reader The Shaft but what I am actually doing is writing *two* books and the first one has just reached The End. In the first one I could be gay and debonair but now I have to change *tone* completely. From this point on my material is no longer comic and trivial but stark human drama, including that account of the gallant and selfless and inspirational deed I promised at the beginning. So if all BB-stackers will drop out here and those serious readers who appreciate that tragedy is the highest form of *art* will stick around we will now proceed.

Incidently, what happened at this juncture was that Ramona, The Scylla of Sex, still submerged and taking bows, was suddenly descended upon in an enormous burst of bubbles by a weird specimen of marine life, a sort of skinny octopus wearing a light cord suit and white buck shoes and shell-rims which, driven by some elemental mating urge, wrapped its long tentacles about her in an ardent embrace and gripping its lips to hers kissed her madly and would not let go despite her writhings until she clunked it over the head with the Pepsi-Cola bottle!

5

Consider this fact: the generosity of our pension plan makes it possible for a salaried person to retire with a high monthly income plus a large cash nest egg to finance lifetime dreams of special travel, a very special home, and other big things that few people can enjoy. This is the financial side of a company which lays heavy emphasis on the importance of people.

RECRUITMENT BROCHURE

Living hell broke loose of course. People in the Full Fathom Deep were clambering over the bar to reach the windows and dying laughing. As we ran upstairs two bellhops leaped into the pool to effect a rescue, not of Ramona, who was okay because of her lung power, but of TV Thompson, who had really been bombed to the bottom by the blow on his head. By the time we made the patio of the San Remo he had been fished out, brought to, and about a dozen characters milled around shouting imprecations at him. For a few minutes it was really Jackson, The City of Action. The upshot, believe it or not, was that Ramona turned out to be very protective of TV, even taking him away somewhere to minister to his wound. The three of us returned to our table to ponder the development, the orchestra struck up, and in a while TV rejoined us, escorting The Scylla of Sex. His suit was drip-dry, so that he was only soggy, but it was obvious, as he introduced Ramona, that his élan was not in the least dampened. He ordered drinks all round and this time I checked a gimlet. But even without drinks and the exhilaration of being at a plush hotel in Florida any four college kids would have been impressed by Ramona because she was, in a word, spectacular. Gads, you should have seen her; pink hair piled in a damp bun high on her head, baby-blue eyes, the brows plucked to nothing and then painted on impressionistically, pink-framed glasses crusted with rhinestones and harlequinaded to resemble the headlights of late-model cars, scads of eye shadow and lipstick, a sheath dress without an ounce of fabric or mystery underneath, and enough cleavage to ruin the North Atlantic Treaty Organization. All she needed to be absolutely Maserati was a chrome rpm indicator at her navel.

"Stupendous act, stupendous!" TV said over and over, glancing down at her terrific lungs. "Used to be in radio myself so I know something about show biz."

"Really great," Ryder agreed. "I do a lot of swimming."

Ramona took a long glug of her double Scotch on the rocks and gave them an incandescent smile. "Thank yoo! It's all a matter of breath controol, yoo have to train yoor loongs."

She had sort of a speech defect, perhaps because, as she told us, she originally hailed from Altoona, Pennsylvania, but probably caused by her habit of curling her tongue and protruding it slightly so that there were a lot of oo-sounds. It was also lascivious. She had been an "entertainer" ten of her twenty-six years, having worked as a singer and dancer. Her most successful act was a double specialty with a comedian who played the xylophone while she did a modified strip and they had worked night clubs as far west as Detroit where she married a big tool-and-die man.

"I'm goin' into communication," TV announced, motioning to a waiter. "That's where the power an' money are. Prob'ly start in New York with one of the networks."

He was drinking fast to restore bodily warmth and not Pepsi-Cola.

"Been in show biz myself," Tuggle said expansively. "At the U. Queen contest practic'ly every week on campus. Member of the court of Homecoming Queen, Miss U, Hon'rary Colonel of the ROTC, Sweetheart of Sigma Chi and Miss Coöperative!"

We had both tried gimlets but I noticed she was now essaying a daiquiri.

"I was oonly nineteen and he was noo big tool-and-die man, he scoowed boolts at some autoo plant. We had an apartment and was I ever loonely having been on the rood. So I bought this darling poodle doog which barked a lot and can yoo imagine what that boorgeois husband of mine did? Had him ooperated on and they took out his voocal choords!"

"Reminds me," Ryder said, "there was this South American kid at Brown, from Paraguay or Costa Rica, a very outstanding type, as a matter of fact his father was the local dictator or something. In any event he came back to school one year with a pet iguana, which is a lizard about five feet long, with orange and black markings."

My dear Ryder was sounding lectury and irrelevant and firing down the Scotch and soda and it struck me we were all becoming rocky except Ramona, and of course me. I had polished off a rum punch and was now testing a pink lady, in honor of her hair.

"May be hicky," I confessed, "coming from a small town'n stuff but I'm not really. I've read my way aroun' the world about a hundred times. My father owns a drug store with big racks of paperback books an's long's I can remember I've been borrowing them t'read. Homer'n Spinoza'n James Jones'n . . ."

"Remooved his choords because he couldn't stand the barking during the hoockey game. That was his one intellectool interest, watching the Detroit Red Wings on TV, what a loowbrow . . ."

"I was a deejay in high school. Had a lousy social life, though, from the wrong side the Jackson tracks, hey, waiters! Ramona, you wanna hear how I got my name, well . . ."

He had two waiters running back and forth with drinks and a bulging wallet on the table trying to impress her while occasional drops of water dribbled down his forehead.

"Nearly made Miss Veter'nary Medicine, I was goin' with this boy in Small Animals, the pres'dent of his class, an' he had it swung for me, I swear, but the Large Animal men, oxen an' things, stuffed the boxes an' some s'rority . . ."

"They climb trees an' run real fast but this one got out of the cage some way in January an' out the house. Somoza, his name was. It was ten below zero'n Providence but we hadda locate him because iguanas don' go for cold climates but then who does I always . . ."

"There I'd sit night after night while he watches hoockey on TV and my lil' doog walking around openin' and cloosin' his mooth and attemptin' to bark and makin' noo sound! A barkless doog! Soo . . ."

"You don' need to travel with paperbacks, greates' invention since Gutenberg. That's why my father had s'many in his store, t'bring culture t'Carter City an . . ."

"Because I was real leprous on campus, Mona, had no group. An' I raped this girl an' sent 'er a TV set to stay in school. I have real trouble with innerpers'nal relations, jus' ask me sometime 'bout is'lation."

"Always a bridesmaid all I've been's made and never a bride. Six times membera the queen's court never a queen! Who knows what a girl has t'do to . . ."

"I lef' that tool-and-die tool in Detroit and took off foor Vegas foor a divoorce and the bright lights again, my lil' boons. Worked the Casbah Hotel in the choorus and then on t'Hoollywood for a coopla years. M'agent couldn' get me a moovie coontract but I did lots've TV westerns as a lapper . . ."

"More books'n my father's drug store'n in the town lib'ry what's this called a grasshopper never had one b'fore . . ."

"We go chasin' through the back alleysa Providence lookin' in trees drinkin' rye to keep warm . . ."

"Y'know in westerns how the heroo goes in the saloon and there's always girls looling around droonkenly on cowbooys' laps, well, they're lappers no cloose-ups or lines but . . ."

"Don' unnerstannit, dating all time'n high school but'n college the competition's so rugged and les' face it, that's why girls go to college to get married . . ."

"Mona you got the mos' triffic body I mean act howsabout goin' out with me, the Mike Todda Mich'gan State . . ."

"People'd ask us what we're doin' an' we'd say huntin' iguanas . . ."

"Didn' like Hoollywood, they're sustanned right to their very sools out there and how you gonna make contac' with a tanned sool . . ."

"Les' hava stinger nex' Tuggle you bitter about TV tryna date her right'n front . . ."

"Can' be well-rounded you never been onna iguana hunt'n Rhode Islan' middla winter an' when we foun' that an'mal . . ."

"Oooo I've seen the seamy side my lil' boons." A real Thespian, Ramona forced from one eye a fat tear which glittered as decoratively on her tanned cheek as a rhinestone. "Yoo're jus' coollege kids and yoo been so clooistered never had a chance much foormal education myself but very fine brain went out with a psychoologist once said my brain must' weigh anyway twoo pounds . . ."

"Not bitter Mer because clue you maybe Quent's the one..."

"Howbout date Mona babyroo..."

"Mistaken ident'y not rich but uncle's loaded . . ."

"Yoo and yoor damn igoona hoont!" exploded. The Scylla of Sex unexpectedly, banging the table with a palm. "Yoo come to Flor'da jumpin' in pools and young booys are dyin'!" She rose suddenly, nearly soaring out of her sheath dress, and raised high one shapely arm. "Down with despoots!" she cried, then sank to our level and beckoned us close. "Give yoo the ben'fit of my wisdoom, my lil' boons. You gotta have dreams and illoosions, somethin' to live foor, whether yoo're in shoo biz or coollege, and I have somethin' want yoo to help. Somethin' to throo yoorself into will yoo help will yoo hooh?" Through her swooped-up frames Ramona transfixed us with a stare until, graped-up and conspiratorial, we nodded. So vigorously did TV assent that he bumped his chin on the table. "Wunnerful, marveloos!" She favored Ryder and TV with a ravishing, sexy smile. "But yoo gotta keep it quiet or the Fed'ral bools will give yoo the hoorn yoo'll graduate from Leavenwoorth University I kid yoo not this is dang'rous top-secret proooject. Now here's the plan I'm on six nightsa week off Tuesdays so nex' Tuesday we all have date okay? Nex' Tuesday night my lil' boons we go into action for causa freedoom and democracy!"

We promised not to breathe a word of what we had plotted on penalty of death, which was simplified by not having the faintest what we had plotted. Besides, we were stoned. Things got kaleidoscopic. TV asked The Scylla of Sex to dance and sort of sogged around the floor with her. Whether it was her breath control or community chest or the number of B.T.U.'s of heat she exuded, when they returned to the table his suit was bone-dry and he appeared physically and emotionally dehydrated. Herbert Thompson had at last met a woman; Ramona had claimed to be twenty-six but Tuggle and I theorized she was at least twenty-eight; as flamboyant as he, and the exposure had been searing and total. Ryder went on describing how they had finally found the iguana frozen taxidermically stiff in the subzero temperature and taken him home and for lack of a better idea put him briefly in an oven to thaw but somehow we never did learn what happened when they took him out. We closed the Full Fathom Deep at two A.M., TV marking our trail with bills. On Atlantic Boulevard we passed The Sheikh's, which was evidently just closing too, for the muddy Mark XX was parked in front and people were piling cased instruments on top. That crazy Basil Demetomos Quartet had sessioned from early afternoon until two in the morning! Now they had stilled the lyre without so much as a place to lay their dialectic heads. At the Shalimar, the boys were so bombed that they were completely incapable of evil maneuver and said a simple, staggery good night. As for Tuggle and I, in our condition we could do no more than shake hands with each other before sacking in, proud of our new purity. I had won my first continent night in Lauderdale and she had lent new luster to her vow. A grasshopper in the hand, we had discovered, is worth a passel of virtuous intentions in the bush.

Incidently, I mentioned earlier that I had eventually managed to make a gift of my chastity to my environment and I had better use that here to segue on to higher things. After the abortive experience with Malcolm and his frigid clarinet in the eleventh grade I bided time till this last autumn at the U. A freshman coed soon claps her dates into three categories. First there is the Wishful Ivy Leaguer who is a fraternity man, very gung-ho about everything, a rank social climber, and who considers himself very philanthropic to have asked you out. Then you have the GDI, or Goddam Independent, who is anti-Greek, in school strictly for the sake of an education, usually majors in Psych, and hates the WIL's guts. Finally there is the Scooter, so named because he hails from a very small town, is very sweet and naïve, loves his home and mother, and misses his little amazingly intelligent pal-dog Scooter. None of these, obviously, would be a worthy recipient of my civic mite; what I had to find was a deserving variation, a boy who would really contribute to society. He appeared in my Core Science lab about a month after classes began. His name was Bobby, he was small and goodlooks, with a cherubic expression which contrasted fascinatingly with his too-long sideburns. We met during one of the first experiments in Core Sci where you type your own blood according to A-B-O and RH, a parlor trick the Core College must feel may come in handy during natural disasters. Hundreds of kids were standing around needling their fingers over glass slides and gaping as the blood oozed, strong boys paling and girls screaming, the whole scene as awful and sanguinary as Grant's Wilderness Campaign. Noting me about to swoon, Bobby bled me delicately, used the anti-serums and analyzed the clumpings. When he discovered we were both Type A and RH-positive it seemed some sort of biological die had been cast. While dissecting a frog in lab the following week we became even more intimate. In this experiment you were supposed to determine whether a frog was male or female, but they were pre-served frogs and their little organs were so fragile and barfy I was damned, once I had sliced open the abdominal cavity of mine; my lab period, incidently, was an eight o'clock, directly after breakfast; if I could tell its oviduct from its ovary. Bobby could. He was a real dream when it came to reproductive systems, being undecided in his freshman year whether to be a chemist or a jet pilot, and he identified my frog as a male and described very objectively how the male buddies around the water on the back of the female clutching her firmly until she deposits her eggs, using as an analogy a motorboat and a water-skier. This of course brought us even closer together and the following week he asked me for a date in the darlingest way: by sending me through the mail several packets of brown and spotted beans and a written explanation so that I could complete a notebook exercise on bean genes for Core Sci in which you guessed if a mating of brown and spotted bean-parents would result in brown or spotted bean-babies. So I accepted and we began going rather steady.

Bobby was very sweet and had a lovely old Nash sedan with glasspack mufflers. We went to dances and football games and became so inseparable that he allowed me to help him with his B-58 Hustler. He was enrolled in AF-ROTC; Air Force Reserve Officers Training Corps; and one of his assignments was to build a bomber model. The Air Force wanted to find out, I guess, if the freshmen boys were *truly* resolved upon a career in SAC. In any event we built a beautiful Hustler together and he got an A on it and that, too, seemed fateful to us. At this point, moti-vated either by patriotism or gratitude, I selected Bobby. He was polite, intelligent, would contribute a lot to society in the lab or the wild blue yonder, was very mad for me, a keeno dancer, and when we made out after a date necked with a restraint and innocent manliness that was refresh-ing. The only thing suspect about his innocence was his tendency to French-kiss given the slightest opening, but this I crossed off to the normal animality of youth.

Despite all rumors, it is actually sort of complex to play house at the U; there are more extracurricular regulations then academic; no boys in girls' dorms and vice versa, more chaperones than guests at parties, no overnight permissions unless accompanied by a doting parent, check in at a hotel or motel and check out of any chance at an education, etc. This leaves the automobile, and the campus police have an enormous fleet of cars which prowl the back roads for miles around, winking red, criminal eyes. So kids have to be ingenious, which Bobby was. When I intimated by means of various, faltering, feminine devices my willingness to allow a semidomestic arrangement, he blushed becomingly but took me on our next date to a drive-in movie. It was early November and cold, but the theater had thoughtfully remained open for the recreation of overstudied student patrons. With the weather so inclement I was surprised at the number of cars. Bobby parked in the next-to-last row, leaving the motor and heater running, and we attached the speaker and sat a few awkward minutes watching the first of the triple feature, a western called "7th Cavalry." Snow commenced to fall. With the swirling flakes and fog from exhausts we could see the screen only intermittently. Inspired at length by Randolph Scott's exploits against the Indians, Bobby suggested timidly we remove to the back seat of the Nash. As timidly I consented. Ensconced upon the ancient coil-springs he embraced me with trembling diffidence, I sighed in surrender and waited. Yikes! You see, with my girlish nobility and self-sacrifice and stuff I had envisioned us a freshman Adam and Eve walking hand-in-hand through the Garden of Passion for the first time, taking childish and experimental delights in the paradise of the flesh, but that damn dissembling Bobby turned out to be a damn *sex-maniac!* No wonder he had known so much about the habits of frogs! No wonder his model had been a B-58 Hustler! Once in his natural habitat, a back seat, he dropped the mask, his eyes slitted, his nostrils flared, he undressed me with all the know-how of a middle-aged lech, and literally bugled the charge! O, it was a real triple-feature orgy. The faces of children appeared through the snow at the windows of the Nash as they munched sleepily on hot dogs and watched with interest the rodeo in the back seat, which must have corrupted them for life. Ironically, it was Bobby's terrible appetites themselves which freed me. Made hungry by his exertions, the sideburned satyr left the car for a hamburger, I clambered behind the wheel and tooled out of the drive-in at high speed, glasspacks throbbing, forgetting to move the speaker from the window and ripping it from the stand by the roots. Back in town I parked by a fire hydrant and in tears and shock found my spastic way on foot to the haven of East Swander. Life, I sobbed, you can starve to hell before I ever again give you so much as a morsel of myself. Ring my bell, base world, and I will be *out to lunch!* Of course, with eighteen's natural resiliency, in a few weeks I relaxed; in fact by the next time a boy called for a date; but from that tragic day, and class, I kid you not, whenever I see a jetstream, cute and evil in the blue sky, I will remember Bobby.

"Do you believe in God, Ryder?"

"Why not? As a matter of fact, I do, but I can't say He rates very high with me as an executive."

"Meaning?"

"Well, in any basic business course you learn that the secret of good administration is delegating authority, which He never has. He tried to make man by Himself when it should have been a team job. Consequently it was botched. No one should take his responsibility more seriously than a member of the managerial class. No, I consider Him okay for a board of directors but I'd never pick such a Being for a key supervisory slot. Anyway, listen to this."

And he began to read aloud to me from several corporation recruitment brochures. It was the next afternoon, the fourth day of the vacation, or was it the ninth or tenth? In Florida time is a blender in which you pour kids and ice and experiences and a bunch of other mystic ingredients and whirrrrr! Who carries a calendar when every minute is a maybe and any hour you could make contact with the *cosmic?* And when it's dark, when the dial of the sun is down, look out, you're lost. So in this book I will ignore the whole arbitrary setup. We were on the beach amid the multitudes and Ryder was lying on his stomach reading while I oiled his dear brown back and were about to have our first lovers' quarrel.

"What slays me is that maybe my profs are right," I interrupted. "About kids today wanting security more than anything. That stuff you're reading, where does it say anything about what kicks a young man can get out of creating a career? According to those corporations all they think college seniors care about is pension plans and how solid they can be financially at retirement. Where's the risk?"

"Thank God the dog-eat-dog days are over."

"Darling," I said, "I just consider it sort of stinky to appeal to a young man on the basis of when he's old. How can you be even interested when there's Couplequip?"

"Couplequip."

"Well?"

He let sand stream through his fingers. "I don't know. But I have to move. My uncle wants a yes or no, I have firm offers from three companies, I graduate in June."

"Are you in doubt?"

"Damn it, Merrit." He sat up with a vehemence unusual in him. "The war aircraft is obsolete and so is the hydraulic system coupling for it and my uncle's made all the money. Couplequip will have to switch over to liquid fuel systems for missiles or stay open as a museum, my uncle knows it but also knows he's too old, he's lost the drive. That's where I enter, if I do. But it's taking one hell of a gamble because a lot of new California companies are there first. New engineering, the whole plant practically retooled."

"What an adventure!"

"I majored in business, not adventure!"

"It would be your own baby!"

"My own coronary!"

"Ryder, what do you want?"

"The Good Life."

"Guano!"

"What's so wrong? Listen, my best offer is a home laundry manufacturer, washers and driers. Stay with them thirty years in the higher echelons and you can clip coupons for a hobby."

"Sure, have a ball at sixty-five!"

He pointed the finger of scorn. "You said yourself you don't dare major in English because there's no future."

Touché. "Ryder, what would you do if you were me?"

"Play it safe. Home Ec or something."

"You mean a woman's place is among the appliances."

"Love me, love my washers and driers."

"Exurbia!"

"You read too damn much!"

"You don't crack a book!"

It hurt him. My eyes filled as he lay face down again with that bitter, invulnerable male majesty a girl cannot fight. The rest of the afternoon was very unsuccessful. The bloom was off the beach. To show my repentance and undying love I continued to oil him but what I seemed to be applying was salt. Once, of all people, I looked up to see Basil Demetomos passing, and panicked for fear he would stop when he saw us, but he went on his moody, muscular way wearing trunks so tight even the kids in the area were scandalized.

"What's on for tonight?" asked The King.

"Tuggle said something about putting on a party at our place."

"I mean with us."

"Nada. I have a date with that musician she was talking about last night. The one from Ohio State with the combo. It isn't really a date, just a meeting, a discussion."

"The Great Books."

"Ryder, dearest, don't be ticked. It was stupid of me and I loathe him."

Half the oil later. "Ryder, what did you think of Ramona?"

"Gross."

The last of the oil later. "Ryder, do something for me, I don't deserve it, but please. This is your last semester, so give up the all-B bit. Try for A's. If you don't it's a waste of talent."

Except for the sound of surf and portable radios and bridge bids, silence.

What actually happened was that we sort of *did* discuss books. During my date, that is, with Basil Demetomos, because the subject came up naturally along with a lot of others. And it *was* a date if his having shaved and wearing a shirt were any indication, but with chinos and no tie so that my slacks were appropriate. He drove us in the gigantic, mutilated Mark XX with the cased instruments on top down to the beach, remarked he had given his men the night off and he himself had nothing more in mind than a walk, so we started, moving along the firm sand near the water. What kicks, I thought, a hike up the beach; later on we can build a fire using no more than two matches, bake a potato and become Second Class Scouts. He grimmed along without a word, having with his short legs to take two steps to my one. Oddly enough we met not another living soul when I had been sure the beach would be crawling with kids on sundry romantic missions and after about ten miles it began to be not a drag but fairly fun. The night was lyric, with a post-card moon and a swell star assortment. After much time The Gloomy Greek deigned to speak. He mentioned The Quartet was staying at the Imperador, which I knew to be even rougher on the budget than the San Remo, and that he had already scouted out two night clubs in Lauderdale which would be glad to have them play gratis.

"I heard the story of your money from Tuggle," I said. "She was the one with Quentin yesterday in The Sheikh's."

"He really emerged with her. But you tell her Quentin's mine. I have too much invested to cross him off to some no-pants with hot palms. She can bed with him to exhaustion for all I give a damn but that's the limit. You tell her."

It burned me. "I will no such thing."

"You better."

"Go to hell."

"Fight?" He stopped, raised his fists and tucked chin into square shoulder, circling me with menace, a welterweight ready to take on a light heavy. He meant it. He snarled.

"Boor."

"But valid."

"Poseur."

"But rich."

"Misanthrope."

"Coed."

Unexpectedly he grinned, cuffed me playfully on the shoulder. "Big girl. I need your Pollyanna personality. I am also . . ."

"I know," I said. "The Playboy Without Joy."

Basil faced the ocean. "England," he said. "Out there."

I waited. It occurred to me one of the greatest things about a Florida vacation was that you could meet and know kids like Basil and Ryder who were really urbane. Most kids at the U have never been further from the nest than Yellowstone Park or Niagara Falls.

We resumed walking. "What I didn't realize," I said, "was how much a hundred thousand dollars can hurt."

"A hundred ten thousand to be exact, after taxes. And it wasn't guilt, you are right, it was hurt. The Telemachus of Toledo, Ohio, with money in lieu of a father and mother and home, love and all that hearthside crock of crap which is nevertheless valid to a certain extent, hoarded up nickel by nickel out of gravy and soiled tablecloths and flyspecks on the silverware. So I gave the restaurant to Uncle Con and headed for Columbus to find a function. Some people find it in God, some in gold, I did in jazz."

"And jazz satisfies you?"

"Absolutely. I think. So long as it doesn't become popular, so long as it stays inconsequential and recondite so that you can give yourself to it without reservation and thus go all the way, so that you can shell it and eat the very *nut*. This you can accomplish if you keep the effort pure by taking no pay."

To me, discussing aesthetics and doing roadwork simultaneously in such a setting was really mystic. His hands were stuffed in his pockets and the moon shadow cast by his misshapen nose concealed half his face.

"So," he said, breathing deep, "that's where the money goes. I've spent forty thousand on the combo to date. That leaves about seventy. I even keep it in a checking account so it won't earn interest, this is a total deal. By the time we all graduate there should be enough left to send us off in San Francisco, which is the Athens of new sounds. Then we'll be on our underivative own. With luck, in other words, and steady spending, I will have purged myself of every dime of that cursed blue-plate-special fortune in two years." He stopped again, confronted me belligerently. "The Quartet is my child, my love, my creation. I feed it, clothe it, house it, educate it, and above all, protect it from the vicissitudes and Laestrygonians. I am serious about its celibacy. I don't mind someone ministering to its animal needs but you tell that Tuggle to have no permanent plans for my piano man or I will set fire to her falsies."

"This is a major night," I said. "I think I'll contemplate it."

He stared as I sat down. "Beautiful," he jeered. "We are a hair north of Miami. A hundred miles north of here is a place called Canaveral and right now they may be launching one into your beautiful night, it may be successful and the contractors will throw a champagne party to celebrate our new achievement in annihilation. Atlas, Titan, Thor, a new mythology with old names! O, the glory that was Greece!"

"And the grandeur that is Grand Rapids," I finished with quiet dignity.

He subsided, finally thumped down beside me on the sand. We sat contemplating, Basil the getting and spending by which his father laid waste his powers, me the pleasure of his unpredictable, radioactive company. How much more stimulating this is, I thought, than sordid sex. O, the life of the mind for me! To our ears came a faraway hum, growing louder. Down the beach a light bobbed toward us, growing larger. Hum and light approached. It was one of those huge imported policemen mounted on his huge motorcycle. We were caught in his headlight beam. He stopped, jammed down his kickstand, cut his motor. With the radio antenna and his uniform and crash helmet he really did look Martian and I half expected him to order us to take him to our cheerleader.

"Yall havin' dahndy fahn tahm?"

"Yes, thank you, Officer," I said sweetly.

"Yall git yur ahss off'n beach'r ah'll run yall in."

"Why?" Basil demanded.

"Citeh ohrdnance nobohdy'n the beach afteh dahk."

"Why not?"

"No scroon puhblic's Law'dale."

I could practically feel Basil's hackles, of which he had so many, rise. "We are *talking*."

"All rihcohlge boh breakhin' beach ohrdnance'n resistin' arres' ahrgue the judge les go."

Basil shot up, hands on hips. "Look, this town is damn eager to have us drive a thousand miles to spend our money and then they gendarme us off the beach, which is what we came down for!"

"Gohdam cohlge kids c'mahn dohwn 'thout no money'n raise hail . . ."

"This young lady and I are having an intellectual conversation and enjoying your well-advertised tourist attractions . . ."

The policeman swung off his seat, swaggered to Basil and loomed over him. It was like Goliath about to massacre a dialectic David. I was very scared but angry, too, and I made up my mind to fight, physcially, if necessary.

"Gohdam egghaids gohn run you in'n cos you 'bout hunnaht dollahs oh the res' yeh vacash'n tahm'n jail . . ."

"How much? A hundred?" Basil stepped back, smiling faintly and cynically. He took out his wallet. "Okay, consider me fined. Only why don't we skip the middleman?"

"You damn cohlge bohs ain't hevah seen no hunnaht . . ."

Basil removed some bills. "The young lady and I would appreciate another twenty minutes' conversation. Five a minute seems reasonable. Here's twenty-five now. You can clock us. Every five minutes step over and collect another installment."

The monster examined the bills. "Ahbedam buddeh allrih you paid up foh fih minniss'n you bettah have nothah twenneh-fih . . ."

Basil took my hand grandly and led me far enough to be out of earshot and we sat down as though nothing had happened. It was very chummy, just the two of us and the ocean and the moon and the policeman and his motorcycle and the occasional southern-accent squawk of his radio, which he was too ethical to turn off.

"What a scavenger," I said. "Of all the mangy deals."

"Remember the oysters? I told you it was a corrupt century."

I said we should go but he insisted, remarking he was determined to squander the money one way or another. So we started the subject of majors and professions and stuff. I explained about my father's drug-store library which opened up whole paperback empires of literature and philosophy and history, etc., to me so that I was reading Silver Badge Original Sexbooks at age ten and the Mentor Nietzsche at twelve. This led into my problem.

"Powdered his feet!"

"He really did."

Police Radio: Students had put a live hammerhead shark in the swimming pool at the Seaserene Apartments, 2901 Federal Highway.

"And I will not be an Uncom. So I'm horned on my own dilemma, a burning desire for knowledge and no major."

"Why not English?"

The law's minion aped over to collect another twenty-five.

"No guts. Basil, what could I do with it? O, in high school I thought about living around the country in a house-trailer and writing basic, obscene novels, but my trouble is, I'm *mad* for lit but I *hate* writers. While they're alive they're so self-conscious."

"Me, too. I mean, hating writers. In England I got saturated with atmosphere and the idea of being an English prof, but who does a more efficient job assassinating literature?"

"I'm such a friction to the U because it's so big and I refuse to relax and fit. I cube up with conscience and stubbornness and when I'm tossed into the machinery it grinds to a dead halt."

"In high school I got very ardent about theoretical physics but look what's happened to science. A trip to the moon or a better can opener."

Police Radio: Four cars with out-of-state licenses were drag-racing in the fourteen-hundred block of Atlantic Boulevard.

"I have to declare myself when I go home, Uncom or English or something, so I have to concentrate now. You know what they say, 'Spring term, when the grass is high enough to go canoeing.' "

"I went on a doctor kick, too, when I first hit Columbus, before I found jazz, but have you been in a doctor's office lately? It's like a one-babe whorehouse, lots of little cribs with sliding doors and the MD slinking from one to another servicing the clients. Prostitution is at least a profession. Medicine is management."

It was time for the third installment. Basil had only fifties in his wallet now but Ahbedam gladly made change.

"The symbol of authority," Basil remarked when we were tête-à-tête again. "Protecting us from ourselves." He drew a long cigar from its plastic tube, lit up, and sent up some preparatory smoke. "That's the bad news for kids today. We are *undramatic*. We have been rooked out of every generation's birthright, which is conflict, which is the essence of drama. The Twenties had a reputation to build, the Thirties an economic struggle, the Forties a world war. We have no damn *contrast*. We have pimples but no suffering, money but no wealth, silence but no depth, artists but no giants, delinquency but no evil, television but no insight, sorrow but no tragedy, roll but no rock, prizes but no rewards, chaos but no anarchy, philosophy but no plan; we have warmth, not passion; dacron, not sackcloth; happiness, not rapture; music, not songs; security, not peace; anger, not rage; cars, not maps; sex, not delight; we have rebelliousness without mutiny, tolerence without love, death without sting, Cinemascope without imagination, challenge without cause, laughs without comedy, vices without sin, individualism without identity, ideals without dreams, contempt without hate, pain without agony; for innocence we substitute naïveté; for nectar, beer; for melody, rhythm; for cowardice, dread; for beauty, charm; for faith, religion; for despair, boredom; for joy, appreciation; for atheism, doubt; for mockery, cynicism; for daring, courage; for sanctity, virtue; for a rack, dissatisfaction; we have extremes instead of limits, we have sweatsox instead of sweat, we have IQ's instead of intellects, we have everything to live for but the one thing without which human beings cannot live—something for which to *die* slightly—not mortally but sufficiently—and we need it so pathetically and cruxially that I am sorry for us to the coolest shallows of my soul!"

Crouched in the moonlight, head thrown back, loaded with the fuel of his youth and strength, he so resembled an Intercontinental Boy-Man ready on its pad to be launched that if I had put a match under him he would have taken off over the ocean, away into the night roaring Canaveral flames from his tail.

"Basil," I said solemnly, "that is the most *way far out* thing I have ever heard."

Police Radio: Riot at Pokey's Bar, 3201 Las Olas, students, ambulance dispatched.

He sank back, lowered his head. "We are drums of skin," he muttered, "and the world beats on us."

"And to think," I said, "if you hadn't been so brutal at The Sheikh's I'd never have known you."

He looked at me. "Big girl, life is glass. At birth they dip you. You have to live within it and no matter how close you come to other people, or try to, all you can do is click surfaces. One day it shatters and you're out. But you're dead."

I looked at him. "No, Basil, you know what I think life is? It's something you carry around in your hand, some tiny living thing. Sometimes you hold out your hand and study it. Sometimes you squeeze it till your arm hurts. When you die it falls, but you don't care. You've had it."

"Tahm's up gimmeh thet las' twenneh-fih yawl stay off'n the beach'n do yeh scroon nice leghal motel'r somewheah y'heah?"

With this parting gem the guardian of law and order took his tithe, kicked his motor raucously alive and we headed for the parking lot. When we reached the Mark XX and Basil opened the door for me he said, "The guy you were anointing this afternoon. Leaguer?"

"How could you tell?"

"They're advertised in the best mags."

"He's very nice."

"Nicc."

He was ruining our entente. He had no right to be interesting *and* gauche.

"You said yourself we have no contrast. I can use a little glamour."

"No guts and no taste," he sneered.

I practically snapped my cap. "You may be a hot authority on youth in general but you can be very stupid about girls in particular!"

"Fight?"

"Take me home!"

"A pleasure, Zelda!"

Parties in Lauderdale are apt to happen whenever you have two kids and three cans of beer. In fact, the third can is not even required. We heard Tuggle's party a block from the Shalimar, and when we got there The Gloomy Greek followed me upstairs out of curiosity, certainly not attraction. Gads, what a blast! The apartment was a mob scene of six-packs and kids in swim suits and Bermudas and sweatshirts, most of whom I did not even know. A portable record player operated in the kitchen by itself and a couple of couples were dancing out on the veranda even though the music was unknown to them. Mostly, though, kids were sitting on the floor boozing and smoking and playing stockrades, a new game patterned after charades. Next to sex, of course, playing the stock market is now America's pastime, but I had not realized how conscious even kids had become. In stockrades you divide into teams, huddle, then each player in turn holds a little sign with a name or word on it while the opposing team, being timed, tries to match the name or word with the name of one of the companies listed on the Big Board, the New York Stock Exchange. Adding up the elapsed times produces the winner. The better you have the listings memorized the faster you can come up with a corporate equivalent. For example, someone held up Ed Sullivan and within seconds a boy shouted the right one, Peoples Drug; the next was Zsa Zsa Gabor, and a girl got her, International Mining. Another easy one was the word "draftees," which was instantly matched with U.S. Gypsum. But they could be tricky. For Eisenhower it took about three minutes to think of Eagle Picher and the combination of Williams-McCullers-Capote stumped one team for five until a literary boy finally remembered Southern Natural Gas. There was a big debate over Jayne Mansfield: the guessing team insisted she had to be Cudahy Packing but the naming team held out for Twin Coach.

"My theory," this boy said loudly enough to pull an audience, "is that the only way to defeat the Russians is to let them defeat us." His sweatshirt proclaimed he was from

Kent State, which he had to be to have such oriental ideas. "Let them come in and occupy. In six months they will be so bogged down in time payments, traffic and tax problems they'll tool out and never darken our shores again. Sure, they'll owe us a lot of money but what the hell?"

"We're a thing!"

"We are eventual!"

It was Tuggle and Quentin, intercepting us as we tried to get beers. Arms about each other, faces beaming, they announced to Basil and me they were in love, had just found out, and wasn't it keeno?

"O, Tug, I'm so happy for you!"

"And without a bed test!" she cried proudly. "And he's an all-A student!"

But Basil, his face swarthy with anger, had Quentin by the necktie. "Traitor!" he thundered. "Give you a night off and look what the hell happens!" He whirled to Tuggle, went into his sparring stance, fists cocked. "He doesn't know what love is, he's just trying to crawl back into the womb."

His use of that word remined me of how Tuggle and I had met in the first place and it also occurs to me I have been meaning for about a hundred pages to stick in something about her background and character, etc. If I seem disorganized occasionally, *c'est la Florida*. She is quite a tall girl with light brown hair originally, I think, and a deluxe figure, though not as out of this world as Ramon's. Her flaw is that if you look her full in the face her nose is slightly crooked, sort of out of joint, like the times. During winter term I developed a galloping case of mono, as did about half the girls on campus, from too many extracurricular activities, about which more later, and was slapped into the U Health Service for a few days' rest. This was the usual treatment, and very successful, except that you got so far behind in your classes that when they let you out you had to hit the books harder than ever and so became more pooped. Tuggle's bed was next to mine. She was also in for mono and an inmate of dear old East Swander but a different precinct, which accounted for our never having met. Her home town was even smaller than Carter City and her parents' only purpose in sending her to college was because the U, they had heard, was a real marriage mill. It was, *but*. Tuggle was too goodlooks for plain boys to aspire to and not beautiful or crafty enough to be a queen or the prey of the sharpest boys. To make matters worse, she was too intelligent to compromise on less than the sharpest. It was a vile deal.

"Exactly the type," she said, "of whom boys say, 'I wouldn't kick her out of bed.' Which is a real southpaw compliment."

In those few hospital days senior and freshman became the best friends we had in school. I helped her peroxide a streak in her hair. She gave me some scoop on how to curl your eyelashes. I confessed what was almost my most secret secret, about Malcolm and Bobby, and she confessed hers. She had played it coy her first two years, then becoming desperate began to sleep around. She kept the awful count in her heart: last year and this she had made ultimately out with seven different boys, to no avail, because now she was about to graduate an El Ed teacher.

"I don't want to teach kids, I want to have them!" she grieved. "I'm just a womb walking around the world waiting to be filled!"

Tuggle was shocked by the ravages of four years in the mill on her looks, the dark circles, the little date-lines. She was almost twenty-two.

"And if you don't have it made by twenty-two these days, you're extinct."

But it was something else which made us bosom buddies forever. One day some of our friends from East Swander smuggled some peanut-butter-and-banana sandwiches in to us during visiting hours; you know hospital cuisine; and they turned out to be her favorite kind, too. Then that night, about two in the morning, we were in the bique eating and smoking and talking about maybe going to Florida together for spring vacation and finding true romance, etc., when Tuggle lowered her voice, "Mer, I won't hold anything back. You'd better know the absolute worst about me. I've had to hide it all the way through school."

"You tell me, I'll tell you."

I thought it must be at least that she was with child or something. Remember, we were both sort of feverish, which is one of the symptoms of mono.

"Mer, in high school I was *salutatorian!*"

"My God, Tug, I was *valedictorian!*"

"You know what my IQ is? *132!*"

"Mine's *134!*"

"Get packed! We're leaving for Arizona!"

"She has much outreach." Poor Quentin blinked, trying

to see through his thick lenses who was slowly garroting him.

"The way they've finally found each other," I said brightly to Basil, "I think it's very *dramatic*."

"Listen, Sophocles, there's a slight drag you've overlooked," snappped Tuggle, a tigress protecting her tiger. "You make San Francisco with this combo and before long your piano man will be playing for the troops in Morocco or somewhere. The draft, ever heard of it?"

"What's the hell's . . ."

"But if he's married and a father he's still yours! Shoot *that* into the tree and see what drops!"

Basil gaped at her, then let go and made blackly for the nearest six-pack.

"He shouldn't drink," Quentin worried.

"Where's TV?" I inquired.

"Probably at the San Remo," Tuggle said, "hung up between Scylla and Charybdis."

"Do you have the foggiest what Ramona's project might be?"

"No and couldn't care less." She clung triumphantly to Quentin's slope shoulders. "But I know what mine is!"

In the game Brigitte Bardot was General Outdoor Advertising, Richard Nixon was Square D, Franco of Spain was Continental Can, but a fight was developing over Norman Vincent Peale. The naming team had picked him as Sunshine Biscuit but the guessing team demanded to know why Joy Manufacturing or American Molasses were not as apt.

Between the bathroom door and the wall heater I ran into Maxine, the motherly girl from Michigan State who lived downstairs with Susy, sipping despondently by herself. "I'm scared, I really am, Merrit," she confided. "Susy's out again with one of the Yalies, she is every night. They rotate. I think they take her to some motel up near Pompano Beach."

"No."

"I'm sure of it. What panics me is that all three of them hand her the same line, that they love her and want to take her away from the provinces and the middle-class ratrace. But I heard them talking by the pool this morning. They called her a punchboard. What's that?"

"I'm not sure," I said, though I was.

"The bad news is that she believes them. I lecture her but she just laughs and says last year a girl from State met a boy from Columbia down here and they got married. She smokes and drinks and doesn't wear her glasses when she can't see her hand before her face without them. So how can she tell what she's doing?"

"Maxine, I don't know. Keep working on it."

I returned to the game with a heavy heart. It was back on the track except in reverse. Associated Dry Goods was Dick Clark, General Dynamics was Bennett Cerf, Swift & Co. was Count Basie's Orchestra, and Freeport Sulphur was Billy Graham.

"There's a chap in India, I forget his name, Behave or something, who wears long robes and walks around the rural areas convincing maharajahs and the other rich they should give land to the peasants, sort of an agricultural Christ." This was from a thin girl with long raffia hair and cigarette-shaped fingers who went to Goosecroft, which I think is a swank girls' school. She blew a rope of vertical smoke and seemed about to ascend it. "That's what I think we should do, kids, you know. Fan out around the country in costume and get people to give to worth-while things like ceramics and road-racing. I loathe the Corvette and I've been through Zen and there you are."

The party began to be uncoördinated. The guessing team had just matched Presley, Sands, Nelson, et al, with Standard Brands when there was a great burst from massed boyish throats. It was The Nassoons, the chorus from Princeton which had come ashore from the schooner, serenading us in formation down in the court of the Shalimar. Cans of beer were dropped to them in appreciation and they went on rendering songs like "Orange Moon," *"Integer Vitae"* and "Old Nassau." Whenever I passed Basil he was drinking from a can in each hand and we would growl something at each other. He accused me again of being craven academically and I retorted he was the coward, jazz was but an escape mechanism. Governor Faubus was Public Service. Our bedroom door was locked and at least three marshy couples were known to be inside. *"Integer vitae scelerisque purus"* sang The Nassoons. Not to be outdone by the Ivy League, the two boys from Illinois who lived across from us announced they would put on an exhibition of diving into the pool from our second-floor veranda. This could be accomplished, they believed, by standing on the rail and giving an extra thrust with the toes. J. Edgar Hoover was Magma Copper. One couple exited the bedroom but two others entered and relocked the door. I caught Basil in the kitchen putting pieces of records into the disposal and accused him of knowing full well jazz is a minor art. "The orange moon of flaming hue," sang The Nassoons, "soars up to cross the Stygian sky." Everyone on the veranda bated breath. The Illinois boy was boosted to the rail, balanced. To reach the water he would have to dive beyond several yards of concrete below. He thrust, soared, and as kids shouted and screamed, arched out and down. He made it. Great applause. Mort Sahl was Ever-sharp. I told Basil he was actually a searcher in search of something major and did not know where to look. I went out to the veranda because one of the Wisconsin boys was about to try the certain-death dive. "Tune ev'ry heart and ev'ry voice," sang The Nassoons, "bid ev'ry care with-draw." The teams had nearly come to blows because the guessers insisted Nelson Rockefeller was Family Finance while the namers' choice was Poor & Co. The storm on the veranda now was the manager of the Shalimar and the tour-ist couple who had the apartment next door whom I have mentioned previously, the Petworths from Long Island, *en deshabille* and *masse*. It was their judgment that the affair was somewhat on the unsilent side for two in the morning. Basil had just discovered Quentin and Tuggle missing and yelled at me where had they gone and I said probably to start evading the draft not that it was any of his business. If we did not break the party the hell up, said the manager and the Petworths, they would call the police.

It was sort of sepulchral when everyone had gone. Bushed, I collapsed on the davenport amid a cairn of beer cans and pyres of smoldering butts. It had been a fine blast, if somewhat disheveled.

I heard a groan. It came from behind an end table. "I've lost him," groaned The Gloomy Greek.

"Integer vitae," I said.

"And you like that Leaguer."

"Don't be obsessive."

"Don't move."

He went out the door and I thought that the finale. I forced myself to empty several ash trays. But he returned staggering, of all things, under his string bass from the rack on the Mark XX. I watched numbly as he unsnapped and fumbled off the canvas case and tuned the instrument.

"Play you something," he said. "I wrote it after I saw you on the beach with him."

"What's the title?"

" 'It's Mystic.' "

He sang to his own accompaniment, his eyes closed, a vein standing out in his forehead with passion, his left hand reaching high on the neck as the bass boom-boom-boomed in the now-silent night:

"Falling in love is a charge,
But it mustn't loom too large;
C'mon, let's face it,
Let's be realistic:

When you're young most songs haven't been sung!
It's mystic.

There's a kick, seeing him yearn.
It's no trick, oiling his burn;
But you're not toiling,
Being altruistic:
Everything's great for the hour isn't late!
It's mystic.

Live it up,
Big girl,
Every day.
Gamble your lips,
And let the chips
Fall where they may!

Squander your heart on dreams,
Though the world's not what it seems;
It's trite but true
You'll be a statistic:
Life's a kite so fly it right out of sight!
It's mystic."

The last thrum of the big bass vibrated through the room. Basil opened his eyes.

"Gee," I said. "That's sweet."

"Sweet." He laid the bass down.

"What's the motivation?"

"You don't know?"

"No."

Again his face darkened, not with rage but frustration. With one foot he moved a beer can as though to dropkick it out a window. He rolled up his shirtsleeves, lifted his hairy forearms in a gesture that might have been classic had he not resembled a Chauntecleer about to crow tragedy.

"Big girl," he said, "I am trying to get through the glass."

"Trying to . . ."

"Yes, goddamit!" he detonated. "And I don't know how! I don't know how to ask a girl for a date so I judo you under the table until you say yes. I don't know how to talk when I do get one so I put up my dukes and offer to go a couple of quick rounds. I'm articulate as hell, I have this terrific vocabulary, but I don't know how to tell a girl I'm cruxially and brain-over-butt in love with her so I have to write a song reminding her how doomed and transitory love and life are in the first place. The playboy who's never played! Except jazz! And I travel abroad and attain the age of twenty-two and silver my temples prematurely and don't know how to conduct or express myself other than to say, Big Girl, I love and lust for every handsome—healthy—sensual—practical—and fecund pound of you!"

I was double-clutched. I had no clue whether to laugh at this midget Tarzan uttering his mating call among the beer cans or cry because he was so ugly and sincere and the third boy within a week to give me the word every girl lives for. This wasn't a vacation, it was a lovathon! But I had no chance to do either for he suddenly, with a shelling of buttons, tore off his shirt, exposing his massive development.

"Not only that, I don't even know how to say I want to have sex with you—here—now—insatiate, omnivorous, Herculean sex—because I'm a virgin!"

"No!" That untranced me. "Not again! No one will ever spring that old soft-shoe on me again!"

"Except for prostitutes," he amended.

"Prostitutes!"

"In London. They're my only experience, carnal, that is."

It was so bestial it might be true. Curiosity tweezed me. If there is any one thing a girl must scout early, it is her *competition*. I sat down on the floor and plucked idly at a string on his bass.

"Basil, what are they like?"

"Professional."

"Be specific."

He hesitated. "Well, in Piccadilly they're young and Boswell. In Soho they're baggy. In Mayfair they're imported from France. They have a certain commercial smile."

"Gads," I said, "how disgusting," failing to add how fascinating. The only other questions about prostitutes I could think of were too embarrassing to ask so we enjoyed a couple of equally embarrassing minutes of silence while he stood over me. Finally I gave an angry tug at the D-string.

"Damn," I said. "Basil, it's not like walking around London. Making your selection. Sex isn't a *cafeteria*. You just can't choose a girl the way you would a salad, say you love her, then expect her to whip out the sofa-bed."

"Oh." He sat gloomily down beside me. "Merrit, are you *intacta?*"

What to reply? How to react? To boys today *no* subject is sacred.

"Sort of," I said.

"Sort of?"

"Twice removed," I said.

"So what's the conclusion? Is sex as salient as it's supposed traditionally to be?"

"I can't deduce," trying to be dispassionate. "Not enough time in the lab."

"Neither can I. Which concerns me because I like to be a little informed in every field." He ran a hand raspingly over his chin. "What is your opinion of me?"

"I think you're very creative."

"Why do girls go to bed with boys?"

"Because they want to."

"I mean, what are the stimuli?"

"Well, they're in love or, though this is pretty unknown though I have heard of it happening, they're knocked out by sympathy and altruism and stuff."

He said nothing for so long I had to look at him, at the thumb nose, the beard stipple, into the bitter-black eyes. "What's wrong?"

"Your frame of reference is the only small thing about you."

"Meaning?"

"You omit the most obvious reason, the most primitive."

"What?"

"And the most fundamental."

"What?"

"This."

With all the deliberate speed of the Supreme Court he reached for me, drew me toward him, draped me over his lap like a heroine in a silent movie, and cradling my head in one hand kissed me as I had never been kissed in my eighteen years. Centuries re-died. Eras expired.

"Big girl, I rejoice in you! That pelvis—infinite enough to mother a generation! Those breasts—glorious enough to suckle a race! That navel—sweet enough to hive bees! Upon you a man might sire a thousand consumers, people all the campuses in the country! You are majestic, Venusian..."

Suffice to state that I found out exactly what her sensations would be: The First Girl To Reach Outer Space. Together Basil and I stumbled upon *dialectic sex,* which may be ancient to humanity but was new to us: the system of question and answer, of Toynbeean challenge-and-response by means of which, if each participant assists the *other* to win, to attain the goal, they can physically and truly go into an Orbit Of Bliss. Exploited in me were capacities and resources I had never known I possessed. Basil discovered he was really a *lover*. Ryder might be charming and efficient, TV emotional and appealing, but the word for Basil was *Homeric*. And when we had finally planted the flag on Olympus, rather than recuperating he rocketed from the bed, switched on the light and went aping from wall to wall on his bowlegs in a state of naked puissance.

"My God, it's great!" he cried in wonder. "Great, great, great! 181226, I love you!"

"And I love you, 360014!"

6

Genes were invented to enable us to explain certain observed phenomena. The concept is a most useful one, and undoubtedly the best explanation yet advanced to account for the particular nature of inheritance. But remember, the gene is part of an explanation, and not a perceivable object.

CORE SCIENCE

After a Lucullan breakfast of instant coffee and herbs because that was all we had in the apartment; she had pulled in around five and it was now noon; Tuggle and I headed for the beach only to become involved in a knock-down-drag-out brawl with the Petworths, who ambushed us by the pool at the Shalimar. A fat, slack-checked pair and real old, at least fifty, they were sunning themselves as we came down the stairs and Mrs. Petworth began jangling her jewelry at us. She had about eight bracelets on each wrist. Mr. Petworth rolled up his newspaper preparatory to striking us.

"I would think young ladies you'd have the social decency to apologize for last night and that we're very sorry worse than high school hoods and delinquents of all the rowdy irresponsible we're very sorry and that smart-aleck un-American game making fun of the President and J. Edgar Hoover and the Reverend Peale the purpose of satire is correction your parents should have corrected you with a razor strop long ago if you have nothing better to do than eavesdrop on parties why don't you read some good books I could recommend several I can't conceive why they allowed you to come down here unchaperoned and carouse around night and day of course they must have let you roam the streets from childhood in the first place I don't see you digging any ditches or baking any bread down here yourselves the point is you don't deserve a vacation because that's all college is today a vacation all you need is a poodle and a box of bon-bons in my day a kid had to work for everything not just have it handed over on a silver platter I'd like to see that damn silver platter just once you're always yakking about drinking and smoking and I suppose the worst kind of immorality get your own kicks lady and quit taking a vicarious trip on ours with the country and the world in such a terrible state it ill-behooves young people what the hell has your age-group done for the world taxes going up and up and the Russians the labor unions you made the century we didn't and I'll clue you none of us voted to be born and the younger generation spoiled rotten cars vacations narcotics bad manners you had the ball getting us and now you can't stand to see anyone else having a thank goodness we have no children of our own they are the luckiest kids on Long Island who the kids you don't have rudeness slang schools full of socialism and I don't know where it's all going to end with a bang lady not with a whimper it's enough to make a civic-minded O go take off in your Cadillac and pass out Taft buttons Communists in the government not only that your husband's a gooser Maxine was going upstairs yesterday and he was right behind her and she told me if I were your mother I'd she wouldn't be caught dead being you I never that's your trouble don't you dare speak to my wife in such gooser O guano!"

This probably did the Petworths more good than all

the orange juice in Florida. There is nothing more vitamin for a middle-aged couple than to have someone else's kids around to bitch at. Tuggle and I understood this so we held no malice.

Incidently, right in the middle of the above conference I remembered that today was my nineteenth birthday.

"I'm nineteen today," I told Tuggle crossing Atlantic Boulevard.

"Grand," she said.

The day went right on being shafty. We were no sooner settled on the beach when the sun aced out behind a cloud and stayed. It was sort of an omen. The thousands of kids ignored it, continuing to play bridge and oil themselves and listen to portables, etc., but they were only role-playing. It was amazing how important the sun was: when you had trekked that far you were really bitter if it failed to show on schedule. You wanted to reach up and claw at the clouds or resign from the universe. What I meant about it's being an omen was that the afternoon really turned grisly when the cell began to assemble. First Ryder appeared in shorts and white sweater and swinging a pressed racket and informed us casually he had just concluded a couple of fine sets.

"Girl from Bennington," he added for my delectation.

"It's Merrit's birthday," Tuggle said.

"Great," Ryder said, "backhand."

"What?"

"This girl."

He looked so defiant and Wimbledon in his tennis rig that I was hit very hard by remorse over our quarrel yesterday and my infidelity last night, and being hit, I knew more than ever that Ryder was the one. Tuggle was briefing him on the party when, to make the deal more dandy, along came Basil gnawing on a cigar and I had to introduce him to Ryder. The conversation roared to a dead halt.

"Merrit's nineteen today," Tuggle said.

"Tough," said Basil.

She made the mistake of inquiring into Quentin's whereabouts and he stared at her so long and with such sad accusation that his cigar went out. Back at the Imperador, was all he could manage, working on new arrangements. He was so obviously in shock over the possible loss of his pianoman to her that my heart, recalling his élan and vocabulary, went out to his ugliness and silvered temples and genius. I became confused emotionally. The day grew darker. A chill wind off the ocean blew us no good. Here and there kids faced it and took off unhappily for the Sand Crab and The Sheikh's. The wind blew us, in fact, TV Thompson. Gangling along the beach, covered only by trunks and a baseball cap lettered Minneapolis Millers, his bare thin chest a mass of goose bumps, he looked so lovelorn and undirected yet purposeful that I felt the same tenderness for him which had been partially my undoing by the Bahia-Mar Yacht Basin. I became even more emotionally confused. Now he would have to meet Basil as Basil had just had to meet Ryder. As he approached, the enormity of the arrangment made my teeth chatter. Not only had I been erotic with all three of them but I had also professed love to all three and meant it in the context of the situation and maybe still did and if they began comparing notes, what a classic confrontation! Merrit of the U in the middle of a quad!

"Friends of radioland," TV saluted us.

I introduced him to Basil.

"It's Merrit's birthday," Tuggle said.

"What's the date?" TV asked.

Nobody knew.

"Well, what day is it?"

Nobody knew that either.

"Well, my God, we ought to be able to pin that down," he said. "Let's pool our knowledge."

We did some brainstorming and agreed it must be Tuesday and then, Basil having found a calendar in his wallet, we worked it out to be the twenty-eighth.

"The twenty-eighth!" everyone said.

We were stunned. We had a moment of truth. The afternoon was killed. That date meant that the vacation was almost dissipated. It was our first terrible reckoning with time. We could visualize our tans turned white. Our ears ached with April gales, we walked in slush to endless classes with profs endlessly challenging. Our story would be written not in sand but in bluebooks. It would soon be over. Here we were, pooping the hours away with problems as yet unprobed, decisions as yet undecided, relationships as yet unrelated; here we were, supposedly having a ball when, at least at instants like this, instants which would come oftener as the end drew nigh, it was all *hell, hell*. For all we were accomplishing, we might as well have been hunting iguanas.

TV sat down urgently. "Listen, if this is Tuesday you

know the score. I was talking with Ramona last night and she reminded me to remind you. This is the night we promised to get her project off the ground."

"We were on the grape," I said doubtfully.

"Who's Ramona?" Basil asked.

"Why should we make points with her for you?" Ryder asked.

I filled Basil in.

"A deal is a deal," TV insisted.

"Yes but what?" I asked.

"I've been wanting to go to Miami Beach and see how we support the rich," Tuggle said.

"She wouldn't tell me," TV admitted. "She says it's too international."

"The Scylla of Sex," Basil mused.

"International!" I said.

"We can cover Miami Beach first," TV argued. "As I get the picture, what we do comes later anyway."

"I won't go unless Quent goes," Tuggle said.

"He's playing tonight," Basil said.

"I'm not getting involved in anything," Ryder said.

TV looked off over the ocean, even its rollers unfriendly. A discarded newspaper flapped over the cold sand, flap, flap. I felt sorry for him. But there was no need: his hands revved, he pushed up the bill of his Minneapolis Millers cap and his shell-rims.

"Listen, you guys gave your word. We're in a groove, it's time we took hold of the petard. Ramona wants as many of us as possible, not a crowd but a manageable team. So let's not chicken out, let's build this a hutch and see what it breeds. We can start about nine tonight, not considering it datewise but an opportunity, and let our intellectual curiosity lead the way, okay?"

"I'll go, TV," I said, moved.

He must have struck a responsive chord in Basil because the muscular one said okay, if it was curiosity and not boy-girl the combo could take the night off. That cleared Tuggle and Quentin. Everyone waited on Ryder.

"Stupid," he said. "As a matter of fact it's vaudeville. It could foul up my vacation. But I get the social pressure so for this one night I'll buy."

So it was unanimous and we adjourned the action to the Sand Crab for beer and congratulations but secretly wondering what unknown cabal we had signed up for. I also got Ryder's message. It was social pressure that put me in

Home Economics winter term at the U. You remember My War With American Higher Education and how, after my visit to the second-grade classroom as a coed observer I dropped El Ed and switched to Home Ec because all my friends in East Swander said I had to, it was the only other socially acceptable major for a girl if she wanted to be nubile. Boys, they swore, were willing to date a Home Ec because they assumed that meant she could cook up a storm, be crack at burping babies and generally authoritative around the ranch-type, etc. So I succumbed. My course schedule for the term was Core Lang, Core Sci, Core Liv, The Vocubulary of Movement; which was really beginning tap dance and the only Phys Ed course I could get into because I registered the last day even though I practically barfed at the thought of tap dancing; then I could elect two of the Home Ec courses open to freshmen, which were The Kitchen and Its Equipment, Health Care of the Family, Interpersonal Relationships, The Consumer in the Market and Family Finance. I heard they were all drags but I elected The Consumer in the Market because it's important for a bride to be able to outfox the A & P and Interpersonal Relationships because I figured I might pick up some college-level lore about handling a husband and also because it was a pre-requisite to another course I planned to take the next year, Advanced Theory and Operation of Appliances. What it turned out to be, actually, was just another of those sad, picky Courtship and Marriage things education keeps throwing at you from the ninth grade to the Justice of the Peace. It was really Mickey Mouse. For example, the prof was a woman, Dr. Raunch, who was in real life *Miss* Raunch, age about fifty, and in whom the vital juices had long ceased to flow. We had a huge, expensive textbook in which she assigned about twenty chapters a week and then we would have class discussions on them, but these, we found, were mainly to educate *her*, not us. The truth was, every coed in that class was more experienced than Raunchy. If a girl happened to use the expression "make out" she tied up completely. The concept of a man's hand on her leg would have been enough to make her miscarry. Most of every period she sat tense and pale while those who hadn't cut out of boredom debated for her benefit such earth-shattering issues as to kiss or not to kiss on the first date, la-la-la. As for casting any pearls of wisdom, Raunchy might better have been out teaching driver-training because although she had probably never been in a back seat she must have been very *wary* in a front.

The debacle came one day when we were discussing a passage in the text, undoubtedly written by some motley bachelor prof. The hour droned on and on and I was already so flaked out from Unirama and Snow Sculpture and Rush Week, about which more later, that I fell asleep and came out of it only when I heard my name.

"What?" I yawned.

"I asked," Raunchy repeated, "for any comment you may have about what our text terms 'random dating.' "

"O," I said. "Well, it is certainly random sometimes."

The other girls died laughing.

She was very bitter. "I have reference," she said, "to the author's observation that it is a 'learning experience' and that 'emotional self-control is essential.' "

"O," I said, trying to up periscope. "I think all that gook is self-evident. I don't think he's been around much. It's like saying we have to have weather."

"If you can lift your language to an acceptable usage-level will you explain that last statement?"

"Gosh, Dr. Raunch, anyone knows when you go out on a date you learn, you have to, but quick. And about controlling your emotions, that's just his priss way of advising us to keep our legs crossed."

The other girls went into hysterics. Raunchy whipped out of her chair, about to crawl up the wall. I hadn't intended to be so flip but I hated to be waked.

"This is an institution of higher . . ." she began.

That burned me. She was being deliberately dense just to pass the time and get the hour over and making me the means.

"We know these things," I argued. "Society's been passing them out on a silver salver since we were twelve. Why can't we try for the giant jackpot issues, for example, should a girl or should she not under any circumstances play house before marriage?"

"Play house!"

Girls were falling out of seats.

"Dr. Raunch, you know what that means!" It was too late to stop, we were on the air. "I'm talking about premarital testing. Who's teaching who? At our stage we need some *lower* learning. And if we can't discuss things like that freely and openly why is this course in the catalogue? We're always being warned about cutting because it costs the U five dollars for every class hour for every student, not counting our tuition. If that's true, with about sixty girls in here and the taxpayers having to put out three hundred dollars for this class every hour, I think it's a crude waste to sit around going through the educational motions! Every hour could buy the U a piano, which some of us really needed last term! I say, let's cut the curriculum!"

The girls were very mute now because I had overstepped the bounds. It's okay to mention money and overthrowing the government and taxpayers and bastardy and down with organized religion and stuff like that in class but bring up the curriculum and you are really trampling out the vintage where the wrath is stored. Raunchy could not even speak for minutes and when she could it was a cross between a shriek and a whistle:

"See the Dean!"

I had had it. She was serious. For about three days they put me on the deanmill, having an appointment with one, being referred by him to another; they practically outnumbered students on the modern campus; being referred by him to another. The upshot was that they allowed me to stay in Interpersonal Relationships but I knew that around Home Ec my name would thenceforth be a dirty word and I would have to switch majors and anyway wanted to because there was nothing solid. Besides, after all this I came down with a lovely case of mono and was shunted into the Health Service where I met Tuggle and we planned the trip to Florida.

The point I kept trying to make to Dr. Raunch and the divers deans was that what we needed in the course was some *concrete* knowledge, not a bunch of abstract, teentime methodology. For example, what is the procedure when you date a jock? A jock is a college athlete, not a fencer or golfer or anything amateur or esoteric but someone really sweaty like a football or basketball player, usually the former. He doesn't have to be a star but he has to be on the squad. On the average every coed dates a jock at least once in her four years and if that seems high, remember the squads are large. Anyway, my big moment came early, during fall term; the Social Chairman of my precinct in East Swander walked in one night and said Ernie Salambo, the tackle, had caught my talent in a Coke joint recently and found out who I was and was now on the phone and would I go out with him Saturday night. I said sure and then, according to tradition, swooned. My roomies stayed calm. Incidently, my two roommates were Linda and Dee-Dee, about whom more later. They went right on studying and smoking and eating as though nothing had happened while I was nearly spastic with excitement. Just as we were sacking in I asked Linda, whom I knew had dated the second-string center on the basketball team, a darling boy but too tall for her, six-ten, which was not his fault but his thyroid's, what was the deal on dating a jock. She said it was a very interesting experience. I said not to be so vague. She yawned and said because of symbiosis. I asked what that meant but she had pulled the covers over her head so I looked it up in my dictionary and found "symbiosis" was biological jargon for "the living together of two species of organisms: a term usually restricted to cases in which the union of the two animals or plants is not disadvantageous to either." This made everything obvious of course.

I got the crude diagram when my buzzer rang Saturday night and I went downstairs and there were *two* boys waiting for me; repeat, *two*. One was Ernie Salambo, who was a monster, and the other was a runty boy with a finger up his nose who stood two steps behind Ernie and was not even introduced to me but who followed us out to Ernie's car, opened the rear door for us, closed it, then slid behind the wheel to chauffeur. He was Ernie's remora. I did not have the term handy then but I did some research later to find examples of symbiosis in nature. Remoras are small fish which attach themselves to the bellies of sharks, eat the leavings of their meals, and offer a kind of unbilical hero-worship. Every jock has one. College athletes have had such bad publicity of late that they have tremendous inferiority complexes and have to gather about themselves any sycophants and morale-builders available. Remoras have the following characteristics: they are so undersized they cannot participate in contact sports, so ignorant they flunk out in a year or two, so barfy to look at they can never get dates on their own, and although not homos so strange that their lasting thrills come from toting team equipment, loitering around steamy locker rooms, and sniffing used shoulder-pads. Also they have unfortunate personal habits such as acne and dandruff. Their lot in life is to end up working in gasoline stations and running out on football fields during games and being ejected by the cops. Yikes, what an experience! For the sake of their egos jocks have to believe that what a girl wants mostly is to be *seen* with them, so a date with one is a series of public appearances. We went to the chief Coke spot on campus in order to sit at the round table reserved by tradition for jocks so that I could display him and his U sweater. Then we went to a movie, being seated just before the end of the picture so that when the lights came on we might be talked about making an exit up the aisle. Then we dropped in at a dance and attracted a coterie of guards, centers, and one fullback although we did not actually dance because Ernie had pulled a groin tendon or something. Ernie Salambo came from a coal-mining town in Pennsylvania, which is where the U gets most of its tackles, was majoring in Phys Ed, hoped to get into pro ball and then be a coach, what else? He kept asking had I seen him take out the end opposite him during the game that afternoon and I had to keep smiling and saying I really appreciated hard-charging interior line play when I actually had not even gone to the game. This was fair because he was just as cagey when I asked him about his scholarship. People who accuse college kids of being rah-rah would be amazed to learn how many of us do not attend the games. For one thing, it's impossible to tell what's transpiring because the stadium is so enormous and the student body gets stinky end-zone seats because the choice go to those who buy tickets from the jocks or are given to alums who never went to college but who are now in the bucks and help the squad with money, cars, watches, apartments, stocks and bonds, clothes, yachts, tutors, vacations, dinners, plane tickets, etc.

To make a long story short, Ernie was a real yo-yo but the operation was not dull because I was so fascinated by his remora. I never did find out his name because he was not introduced and did not speak. He chauffeured us everywhere, served our Cokes, lit my herbs, bought our movie tickets, ushered us to seats, checked our coats at the dance, etc., all the while gazing at his hero with the same man's-best-buddy, adoring, beatific expression that must appear on the faces of the meek when they finally get to God or tycoons when they finally meet President Eisenhower. Surreptitiously he also gave me the gaze. Jocks' dates are as close to real dates of their own as remoras ever get. He was a lamb, except physically. He looked like one of those specimens plumbers find alive under old sump pumps and take to zoologists to be identified.

When we left the dance and were in the car with the remora behind the wheel Ernie Salambo said:

"Wangooutncountrynscrew?"

"I guess not, Ernie," I said. "Your groin."

"Oke."

If there is any one thing jocks gain from athletics besides an education it is sportsmanship.

"Wanstayherenneck?"

"I guess not, Ernie," I said.

"Oke."

So the remora drove us back to East Swander, parked, and shuffled respectfully two paces behind as Ernie Salambo escorted me toward the door. About a hundred couples were deployed among the shrubs and against the wall writhing through the good night ritual. Ernie loomed. All at once I realized I had charged head-on into a crisis. A good loser on every other point, he expected a farewell kiss. I had no desire. I was even reluctant. Yet a semi-star tackle would drop all kinds of caste if he were seen sloughed off before a dorm door. I hadn't the faintest what to do because I had not yet taken Interpersonal Relationships. In the next minute the tableau became very taut, including several nearby couples who paused to observe and refresh themselves.

Then in the semidarkness I saw Ernie's remora waiting patiently for his master with his finger up his nose, and on a sudden inspiration of sympathy for all the remoras of the world, dumb, loyal, midgety, unloved, who have waited thus through time immemorial, I went to him, threw my arms around *him*, and gave him an accolade that practically tore off his lips.

7

Answer yes, no, or ?, but avoid the latter if possible: 1. You would rather be a forest ranger than a dress designer. 2. You often wonder why people behave as they do. 3. You are much concerned over the morals of your generation. 4. You feel deeply sorry for a mistreated horse.

BOBB TEMPERAMENT TOTALIZATOR

"Viva la revolootion!"

We all sat like bumps while The Scylla of Sex tossed her pink head proudly and passed around her flashiest smile.

"La revolootion, my lil' boons!"

We went on gaping, which was par for the course that night. Except for Ryder, who was naturally debonair being League, and Ramona, who had mothed around the bright lights for years, none of us; me or Tuggle or Quentin or TV or Basil; had ever felt so hicky. The seven of us had driven down from Lauderdale to Miami Beach in the Mark XX with the string bass on top, Tuggle and I in heels and our best dresses and the boys in their neatest suits. This was to be our big night on the town. Now everyone has read about and seen pictures of Miami Beach but until you have witnessed it in person you have no scope. First we took a quick spin past all the fabulous hotels and night clubs and things, then parked the car and window-shopped Lincoln Road. Ramona acted as tour conductor. I have never seen such fabulous sheets of plate glass, such fabulous furs, such fabulous jewels, such fabulous people. They would never believe me in Carter City. I go all-out for capitalism and free enterprise and Tippecanoe and Tyler Too; my father owns his own drug store and I know how he has to slave over the books and inventory and the prescription counter and I would fight anyone or any ideology which tried to ace him out of it; but I clue you, class, then and there I began to develop a sense of social injustice. Also, I was nineteen that day, remember, and beginning to feel ethical. But let's face it: who really *needs* a diamond choker for his hairless Chihuahua? If someone that minute had slipped me a pledge card for the I.W.W.'s I would have started picketing. At the very least, I would pass a law stating that everyone who winters in Miami Beach must bring along someone less lucky as his guest, someone like old Mrs. MacIntyre who lives down the street from us and has outdoor plumbing and can barely make do on her Social Security. Miami Beach is too fabulous not to be shared.

Next we had drinks at different famous hotels, the Deauville, the Americana, the Internationale, the Fontainebleau, with TV and Basil picking up the checks and Ramona introducing us to such new taste sensations as gin Hialeahs and red snappers. If it was part of her plan to have us all somewhat smashed, she made it. We wound up in the Coq d'Or Room of the Biscania at a table overlooking an illuminated pool and many palms and a hedge of silver cabañas, with beyond them the black void of the Atlantic.

"What revolution?" we demanded.

She rose melodramatically, bent over us, exposed to the boys her terrific lungs, blazed her baby-blue eyes, extended a shapely arm toward the window, pointing over the cabañas and pool to the black ocean.

"There!" she hissed.

Then we remembered. They were having a revolution in Cuba. Most of us had seen stuff about it in the papers but had paid no attention because we were making our own current events.

"So?" Ryder said. "They're always having one. Local color, pulls in the tourists."

"Ooooo!" Ramona swayed down savagely. "Yoo out hoonting igoonas and two hoondred miles from here young booys are dyin' for freedoom and demoocracy!" She made us huddle. She told how an intrepid band had landed on Cuba's coast, how their ranks had been augmented by hundreds of youthful patriots, boys and girls both, how they were holed up in the mountains of Oriente Province, lashing out in guerrilla raids, retiring to bury their dead and grow beards, sometimes having nothing to eat but python meat. She made it as picturesque as a tropic, coeducational Valley Forge.

"But who are they fighting?" Tuggle asked.

"Where've yoo been?" Ramona asked.

"College."

"Don't any of yoo knoow?" Ramona appealed.

We shook our heads.

"Batista!" she hissed, slitting her throat with a pink fingernail.

"Let's dance," Ryder invited me.

His timing was sort of impolite and to show my displeasure after we were on the floor I said I wished he would not let TV and Basil pick up every check.

"They enjoy it," he said. "Fighting over the tab has never indicated good breeding."

"How nice," I said, "that good breeding is also economical."

We danced.

"You really appreciate this Basil The Most or whatever it is?"

"I think he's very unique. Also possibly a genius."

We danced.

"I had a terrible time last night, Merrit. This girl from Bennington, very avant-garde and all that, including dirty ears, then this morning we played tennis. I lied when I said she had a great backhand. She showed at the court with a racket with no strings, which she said was symbolic. What a weird game, me serving and her swinging and the ball whooshing right through her racket and her running around shagging balls until she nearly had a coronary. She said kids today don't suffer enough. Those damn Bennington girls."

We danced. Then he led me down some stairs to the pool and behind the nearest silver cabaña. He said his date had been a drag because, besides her unwashedness he had thought of me constantly, missed me, loved me. He said he did not want to seem negative about things but I had mixed him up with a lot of types new to him.

"A songwriter, an underwater dancer and revolutionary, a jazz piano player, this Thompson big-talker— I've never mingled with people like these. They just don't hang around Brown."

"Symbiosis," I said. "It may be healthy for you."

He gripped my shoulders. "But I'm out of my element, Merrit! I can't adapt!"

There was enough light so that I could see the seriousness in his brown, bedroom eyes. He had never been more handsome.

"You have to, Ryder," I ultimatumed softly. "You have to be Jaguar and come-what-may and live up to my illusion."

"I'll try, but my God, Merrit, you're not making it easy! Do you realize we only have three more nights in Florida? Three more nights to be together? That adds up to three more days to decide about Couplequip! I came down here to go stag in my uncle's house and think it through and you make me fall in love and involve me with this eerie troupe and sleep with me once and say you love me but no more sex! Well, if you want me to Fitzgerald you have to follow through! I'll volley but I have to have strings!"

I understood. It was cruel and unfair of me to demand and deny simultaneously.

"Ryder, dear," I whispered, "I'm so sorry."

He held me close. "And you love me, darling?"

"Oh, yes."

"And you'll sleep with me again? Tonight?"

"Yes."

Perfect kiss.

Back in the Coq d'Or Room at our table Ramona was

throwing every crime in the book at the dictator Batista. According to her he combined the sterling qualities of Caligula, Ivan the Terrible, Hitler, Mussolini, Farouk, Stalin and Mickey Cohen. Her tongue tip darting and dripping venom, she described his suppression of civil liberties, his leeching of the treasury, his system of informers, his secret police and their clever innovations at torture. But her angriest indictment she saved for the American people who, with the dirty dishes of tyranny piled practically in their sink, went on watching Perry Como. She was so bitter that if she had been in a pool, no matter how large, they could have advertised it as heated. I can't say we were enthralled. Tuggle and Quent held hands, not dancing because he had never learned how, having played professionally since age twelve. Her best audience was poor TV, who nodded and opened and closed his mouth without making a sound and who was obviously so sick, sick for her that his nose must have burned. But now, she climaxed, it was Batista's turn. In the last two years our neighbors to the south had flushed Jiminez of Venezuela, Perón of Argentina, and Pinilla of Colombia. Fulgencio Batista had to be next.

Basil asked me to dance and I accepted but no sooner had we gone into formation than he stepped on my foot with such finesse that my plastic, high-heeled springo-later sprang right off and while retrieving it from other couples he said let us get the hell out of there. We used the same exit Ryder and I had taken and in a minute were down by the Biscania pool and vanishing behind the same silver cabaña.

"Even if I could dance I would draw the line," he said. "That band. Violins. I suppose they use old Haydn arrangements."

Incidently, he wore a silk suit which must have been murderously expensive but which did a lot for his looks.

"I don't even know where Archie and Ray are," he said darkly. "Probably on dates or auding records. And Quent being made before my eyes. And that pink-head *provocateur*. I might better be somewhere bobbing for apples."

"Thanks," I said.

"And this Leaguer," he said, putting a hand against the cabaña as though, like Samson, to topple it around the Philistines. "If I ever went to a B movie, he is. I know the type. A martini mind and a buckle-back soul."

"I did not come out here," I said with some hauteur, "to have my friends insulted. Besides, you're jealous."

He stalked me. "Jealous, hell yes, and insulting and ugly and ill-mannered and Greek—but also real and semi-mature!" He seemed about to be brutal, as was his wont, but surprisingly, through sheer will, restrained himself. His voice took on a strange, almost a spiritual tone. "But I'm also perceptive enough to recognize that what happened last night was the finest experience of my life. Big Girl, wasn't it yours?"

This was a new Basil Demetomos. I had to be straight-arrow. "Yes, it was."

"And do you know why?"

"Why?"

"Because it was valid. That, today, is the rarest. If you can find validity in sex or life or anything, hold it. We should stay in the sack and send out for meals. I was figuring, we've got three more nights after tonight, three. I should fly with the flock, guiding us toward our own sound, but I'm willing to sacrifice because what we achieve together on a Simmons is greater progress. Now I'll tell you and ask you."

He moved close and elevated himself so that our eyes met. We touched, yet he did not lay hand one on me. Far above us glittered stars and the lights of the Biscania. Distantly there was music, and traffic sound, but through these, penetrating, hot-tempoed, the boom-boom-boom of Basil's heart rocked me.

"181226, I love you. Shall we be valid tonight?"

Thanks to everything, including the grape, I knew not what I did or said. I was caught up in the dialectic of the universe.

"Yes, Basil."

Like children, hand-in-hand we returned to the Coq d'Or Room. Ramona was describing how Miami had become the overseas headquarters and arsenal of the revolution. There were 85,000 Cubans in Dade County and all were in the underground. They raised money any old way. Waitresses donated tips, salaried people a percentage, grade-school kids their pennies. With the money agents bought machine guns and rifles and bazookas and mortars and grenades and ammunition and medical supplies all over the U.S., which were shipped to Miami in cars, trucks, housetrailers, even suitcases, where they were cached in apartments and car trunks, even buried in sand dunes. The big problem was how to get them across to Cuba. The area was crawling with very mean and tricky FBI men because it was illegal to supply arms to foreign powers. Arrests were made almost daily. Somehow, though, the goods were moved. Planes and boats were hijacked, loaded on unused airstrips and along the labyrinth of waterways, and slipped out by night. It was an endless, exciting game of cops-and-rebels, only grown-up. And the ironic hooker was that here, in the U.S., in the land of the free and the home of the brave, etc., people had to go underground to fight for liberty. "Of coorse," she said meaningfully, "oodles of Americans help, too."

TV nodded with such force his shell-rims banged up and down. "Let me give you the scoop on this Phi Bete from Minnesota hitch-hiking I picked up on the way down." And he launched into the story he had told me in the Sand Crab. "How many kids at your schools do you know would slough everything for the sake of an abstraction?" he ended. "I tell you, what that guy was doing, and I use the word with great care, was *epic*."

"Epic?" cried The Scylla of Sex, who was becoming stoned. "It was histoorical!"

TV ordered another round.

It suddenly struck me that I had promised two boys the same thing at the same time.

"We need moore of everythin', thoogh," Ramona pursued. "Planes an' weapoons an' boots an' . . ."

"Ryder's got a boat!" Tuggle announced brightly.

It was a real faux pas. She never would have said it except for the red snappers. Everyone went rigid. Ramona's face turned pastel as her hair.

"Yoo do?" she breathed.

"You do?" TV said.

Ryder could have choked Tuggle. "I do not. My uncle has. And it goes up north next month."

Basil, bless him, got us back into gear. "Ramona," he said, "why are you so knocked out by this Cuban thing?"

"I'm glad you asked her, Bas," said TV, being very Rotarian. He and Basil, at least, had established a rapport. "Glad you asked her."

Drinks came and Ramona chug-a-lugged hers while the orchestra played "Moon over Miami" before replying. "I tol' yoo," she began, turning pinchbottle serious. "Sing a lil', dance a lil', moodified strip, an' noow this pool bit. But what've I got but my boody? N'en I come to Floorida an' there's a revolootion an' for the firs' time have somethin' to live for as a hooman bein', somethin' to throow myself into an' alsoo my brain an' I have a ver' fine one, this psychoologis' says it weighs anyway twoo pounds. But thas' neither here noor there." She dabbed at her eyes under the rhinestoned harlequins. Her Scotch underground was really operative now. "Cuba's the woorld in microocoosm, lil' boons! I could be out makin' a minka month but am I, noo! Ten percenta my sal'ry at the San Remoo I give to the revolootion! Soo kids, when yoo see Ramona in 'at pool thas' joostice she's drinkin', not Pepsi-Coola!"

"Amen," TV said solemnly.

"Ugh, python meat," Tuggle said. "What is it you want us to do, Ramona?"

She told us. In Miami proper there was this big night club called the Caribbee, which had a continuous floor show and the owners, being sympathizers, every Tuesday night allowed outside acts to perform and take up collections, the money to go to the revolution. This was one of the means by which the underground raised funds. There were always lots of Cuban acts, she said, but the patrons would contribute more when Americans performed, and that was what she wanted us to do, get up and sing our various school songs, that was probably all we could do, but as college kids we would be cute and winning and the clientele would really dig down for us.

"See how simple, friends?" TV said. "I told her we'd be glad to, for the cause!" He grinned evangelistically.

There was no warmth at all. It was not a breakdown in communication or because the whole project seemed strange and oriental, our coming all the way to Florida to sing in a night club to make money for a revolution. It was just that, as I mentioned earlier, college students today are fresh out of response. We are allergic to challenge because we are the targets of so many: raise your grades, drive carefully, cut that hair, learn to like good music, shape up and save the world, improve your morals, etc., to list only a few. So we sort of lounged and enjoyed the luxury atmosphere of the Biscania while Ramona and TV waited. After all, we *were* on vacation. Besides, TV had become a stooge to love and Cuba was beyond our field of interest.

"It's immature," Ryder said, settling the issue.

"Doesn't Brown have any good songs?" Tuggle asked.

"Party-pooper!" said Ramona.

"Leaguers live off immaturity," Basil said.

"What's that mean?" Ryder demanded.

"It means," Basil flared, "that you guys come down here on the New Haven Railroad and con immature coeds from the Midwest into believing you might marry them! On condition they hop in the hay!"

"I resent that!" said Ryder. "For Merrit!"

"Resent?" Basil snarled. "Is that all you get from those charm schools? Don't they teach you how to get gut-mad?"

"Go run a restaurant!" Ryder said.

That really blew up the isosceles triangle. The regional war resumed, the one in which TV and Ryder had fired the first shots at the San Remo. Basil called Ryder decadent and Ryder called Basil bourgeois. Basil said Brown died with transcendentalism and Ryder said at Ohio State you could major in Restaurant Management. They staged such a scene that all the big spenders at tables around us stood up to watch and waiters commenced hovering and the band, on signal, struck up "For He's a Jolly Good Fellow." I was afraid we would be bounced. It was all my fault, actually, for slipping out to the same cabaña with both of them. Now they were on their feet.

"You crude crud!" Ryder said.

Basil went welterweight, fists up, chin tucked into his shoulder.

"You ethnocentric sonofabitch!"

"Oooooo, yoo lil' adoolescents—yoo stop or I'll spank hell out of yoo!" And Ramona rushed between them raging, a Miami Beach Madame Defarge waving a double Scotch instead of knitting. "Hoow dare yoo!" she cried. "Yoo and yoor lil' hates an' looves! When out there," pointing toward Cuba again, "booys are spillin' their bloood for hoomanity! An' yoo won't even sing a soong for 'em! Shame, shame on yoo!"

Her timing was terrific. Basil and Ryder unCoq'd. And just as she was making them shake hands, Quentin, who had not been heard from all evening, raised his red snapper and croaked:

"To the ultimate!"

"He means," Tuggle translated, "to the Caribbee!"

So we actually did go after all, sort of despite ourselves, not because of *Fidelismo* or the boy from Minnesota but because Basil and Ryder were slightly ashamed of having made themselves *conspicuous* and mainly because we were bored by this hour with the Biscania. Also, for kicks. When we were just piling into the Mark XX Basil stopped us and asked TV to drive. We could not, he said, do anything in public as cornball as sing school songs. In the interim he would call upon his muse and see if he couldn't create something clickier. So over the causeway to Miami we tooled, TV driving, Ramona directing, and everyone being very noiseless while Basil smoked it up with a long cigar and scribbled on paper under the domelight and hummed to himself.

He remained creating in the car in the parking lot when we reached the Caribbee and Ramona took us in and staked out a table and conferred with the management. She then told us all arrangements were made and we were booked to go on in an hour, about one-thirty A.M. The Caribbee was dark and enormous and loaded with *turistas* who were loaded and every waiter was Cuban and the bar was lined with mustaches and white teeth. We felt part of a real-life situation. It was sort of thrilling. The floor show was already under way, featuring that night Ubeda I and his Marimba Band, consisting of three marimbas, one trumpet and a set of bongo drums, all of them wearing tight pants, patent-leather hair-do's, and exotic frilly-sleeved shirts. They were out of work but very acrobatic and prone to shouting *"Olé!"*, particularly while playing a thing called "Castro's Cha-Cha-Cha." I suddenly realized I had promised two boys the same thing at the same time. Ubeda I was a buddy of Ramona's and came to our table but since we were not bilingual there could not be much plotting.

Then Basil called us out to the parking lot. He had produced a number for us and one for Ramona and getting his bass from the top of the Mark XX he tuned up and rehearsed us right there on the tarvia amid all the cars. Both of them were keeno. Even Ryder was impressed. Then we returned and after a dance team and a monkey act it was our turn. Ramona broke the ice, Basil accompanying her, and after some casual patter with him she did his number, which was titled "The Curse of a High IQ." We could tell at once that The Scylla of Sex was a real professional. With her glasses off and her slinky black dress and fabulous figure she was really aphrodisiac, yet her smile was so broad, her bumps and grinds so exaggerated and raffish that we nearly died laughing. This is what she sang:

"Chicks—listen to my advice;
I've lived and learned—at a price.
To be born with a brain is a pain
When the male of the species doesn't give a whoop
in hell if you know enough to come in
out of the rain!
Yet—
Seducible or rigid—
Passionate or frigid—
Platinum or auburn or brunette—
Here's a message you had damn well better get!

The curse
Of a high IQ,
Is the worst that can happen to you;
Reveal you have a head,
And romantically you're dead—
So play dumb whatever you do!

Don't mention Quemoy
To a boy;
Avoid
Any talk about Freud;
A wise chick eschews
Discussion of news,
Don't stick out your necks—
Stick to sex!

Those with a mind
Will find,
That ignorance is bliss,
So here's a clue:
If you want to be molested—
Keep your intelligence arrested!
From high school to the hearse—
For a girl there's nothing worse—
Than the curse
Of a high IQ!"

She got great applause and made Basil take a bow and then called us onstage and had us each announce our name and school. Then grouping us around Basil and his bass she introduced our number, "Glands!", and we were on our own. TV held the word-sheet, Basil lit a cigar and gave us the beat. If I do say so myself, we were okay. The drinks gave us *esprit* and we made practically no fluffs. "Glands!" was part song and part Greek-chorus and we alternated chanting and taking solo turns on the verses. This was it:

"Since man evolved
From elemental ooze,
To adolescent conduct
He's sought clues:
How explain through centuries of unremitting
scientific research—
Activity of a carnal nature which begins in
back seats and ends,
alas, infrequently in
church?

The answer is,
Of course, eclectic;
Not to be found
By method dialectic:
Inscrutable to geology, philology, biology,
mythology, tautology, and
similar disciplines flimsy—
But shockingly obvious to anyone with sufficient
intellectual curiosity to open Kinsey!

Why does animal life abound?
What's faster than the speed of sound?
More flammable than rocket fuel?
Irrational than The Golden Rule?

It isn't the sea,
It isn't the sands,
It's no mystery—
It's glands! glands! glands!

What's the reason why our youth
Is uninhibited and uncouth?
Why does the younger generation smolder?
Seem more frenetic than the older?

It can't be contained,
In bottles or cans,
It can't be explained—
It's glands! glands! glands!

Why do we tool off somewhere tropic?
Is our vision of the world myopic?
How do we manage sublimation
Of all the problems of the nation?

It's not that we're bored,
With issues or stands,

It's nothing abhorred—
It's glands! glands! glands!

Why are we dulled with study textual?
Obsessed with every pleasure sextual?
Psychotic over jazz progressive?
Is something in our genes recessive?

It isn't the bust,
The chest or the hands,
Deduce it we must—
It's glands! glands! glands!

Why do we adjudge our homes
Less crucial than our chromosomes?
Why is our behavior spastic?
Indicative of a code elastic?

Let us clue you in,
Our middle-aged frands
Don't label it sin—
Because it's glands! glands! glands!

Is it—

Ritual?
A more precise term would be habitual.
Procreative?
Perhaps. The purpose, however, is recreative.
Terminal?
Only by accident. Though it's certainly sperminal.
Reprehensible?
Depending on the point of view. To us it's sensible.
Laudable?
Difficult to say when it's scarcely audible.
Sentimental?
Under no circumstances. Purely experimental.
Bestial?
Impossible when the most favored lighting is celestial.
Then what is this cosmic force that no one understands?
Is it uniquely American or operational in all lands?

Well?

Hell!

It isn't the sea!
It isn't the sands!
It's no mystery!
It's glands! glands! glands!

Well, class, it was a triumph of group dynamics. We were taking bows and grinning like apes and thinking of careers in show biz when Ramona made us quick scatter and collect the tribute while the place was still in the mood. We moved from table to table and reassembling at ours counted the take and found we had garnered $219.21! Ramona said that much would buy two Garand rifles and some "amoo" or, even better, one WW II .30 caliber machine gun and we had better move on to the collection point. So, following her signals, we took off in the Mark XX again, this time winding up in a small all-night restaurant in downtown Miami where, she told us, we would somehow get the word how to turn over the money and also where we must keep a sharp lookout for men wearing innocuous ties, hats, white shirts and Sherlock expressions, who were sure to be FBI agents. Since we were ravenous we crowded into a booth and had hamburgers and French fries and malteds and stuff. Our waitress, we noticed, was Cuban and one of the short-order cooks sported a large mustache. Before our order came The Scylla of Sex and I went into the bique to redo our lipstick and while at the mirror she said innocently:

"Hoo big is yoor booy friend's boot?"

"Fifty-five feet, I think."

"Ooooo, a real Mooretania. Where is it?"

"TV's in love with you."

"Amoor, amoor."

"He's very young. You're a woman of the world."

"I noote yoo have two on the hoook, child. Where is the boot?"

"I like him a lot, Ramona. I couldn't bear to see him bruised."

It was a feminine draw.

I clue you, devouring a cheeseburger and watching for FBI agents really makes the digestive process *interesting*. Among her French fries Ramona found a one-word note, "car," so when we paid our bill and went out to the Lincoln our little Cuban waitress followed us and said she was the pickup. We gave her the two hundred and she nearly broke down with gratitude. We left the area in a welter of altruism and self-congratulation. Her timing terrific as usual, Ramona said she had decided to have a cold the next night, which was a legit excuse not to be underwater, and would we like to do something else for the revolution, no performances, just a fun way to raise more money? We said sure, *c'est la guerre*. The rest of the trip to Lauderdale the six of us kids were silent. The fact was, we were embarrassed by how selfless and humanitarian and way far out we felt. It was not really Cuba or *integer vitae* or striking a blow for freedom or any of that jazz but that we had proved, even on vacation, that college kids today could submerge personal differences and idiosyncrasies and regional resentments and really *coördinate*. This was sort of unknown. At the same time I started to panic. One date with destiny is tough enough but two were impossible. And Merrit of the U had talked herself into a *ménage à trois*.

It was so horrible I do not know how to put it on paper.

Back at the Shalimar.

TV and Ramona roaring off in the yellow Porsche.

Ryder and Basil stalking me.

Tuggle and Quentin clinching.

The pool, beautiful, rippling.

An underwater floor show.

A small figure in a swim suit.

Blonde ponytail like seaweed.

One arm tied by a nylon to an aluminum chaise longue so that the small figure, no matter how it struggled, could not surface.

Susy, The Suicidal Mermaid.

I screamed.

Ryder was first into the water, lifting her up but unable to completely until Basil leaped in and heaved the chaise longue out as Tuggle and Quentin came at my scream. The boys stretched her on the grass and began artificial respiration and cut the nylon stocking. She couldn't have been in the water long, it had still been rippling from her struggles. O, God, God, God, it was horrible! It was like a baby being run over by a Good Humor truck. In a few minutes Susy was breathing and gagging and crying she didn't want to live and we carried her into her efficiency apartment and rammed out the sofa-bed and got her into it and sent away the manager and other tenants who had been waked by saying she was okay, she had just fallen in the pool. Maxine came back from what had been her first date in Florida and went into hysterics. We made coffee for Suse and made her drink it and sent the boys out so she could tell us what had happened. Between shame and crying the poor little thing was practically incoherent. It was as Maxine had feared. It was the three Yalies, in rotation handing the innocent sophomore from Michigan State the ancient line about marrying her and taking her away from the Sinclair Lewis section and in the meantime making her a punchboard, the beasts. Tonight Dilworth, the one I had heard through the wall, had taken her to a motel for some shack and got her drunk; enter the other two, who tried to make a kind of obscene round-robin out of it. Finally, when she became hysterical, they brought her home. Susy knew at last what she had done and what had been done to her. She had gone to bed, then risen, put on her swim suit, tied herself to a chaise longue, shoved it into the deep water, dragging herself under.

Tuggle and I were so furious we ran out to the Yalies' apartment but the door was open, lights on, and they had moved out, damn them, evidently fearing retribution.

If we had not put on the show at the Caribbee we might have been at the Shalimar and Susy might not have made the try.

If we had not reached the Shalimar when we did she would have drowned for sure.

Her words, the first day I met her; that if she could have a date with a real Ivy Leaguer she'd be ready to die; were tattooed on my brain.

We talked with them about two hours while the boys waited dripping. Susy wanted to go home, not to school but to her mother and father. Maxine did, too, but they had no money and their ride to Michigan would not leave for three days.

It was four in the morning by now. We helped them pack. Basil then drove the seven of us to Miami International Airport, bought two tickets to Lansing, Michigan, and we put them aboard the first flight out. Neither of them had ever flown, so there was some consolation. We drove back to Lauderdale as the sun rose unreally. No one said word one.

Tuggle and I collapsed in bed but I had too much nervous tension to sleep. I couldn't cry any more. When I closed my eyes there was the pool, and in its lovely deeps, pendant, a mermaid with a ponytail. For me, for the rest of my life, every pool would come equipped with one.

Florida had been a ball but the ball was over. Nothing would be quite as lyric henceforth. From diamond dog chokers and red snappers to revolution and near-tragedy in one night.

A girl I *knew* had actually attempted to *kill* herself.

And whenever I thought of the parallels between Susy's situation and mine I panicked. There had been three boys in her case, there were in mine. She had played house with all three. So had I, with one at the identical corrupt motel. And only her sad, suicidal deed had saved me tonight from a double entendre of my own. We were both from small towns, had never really traveled before, and were both amateurs at the roulette of the heart. But why, why, why had Susy lost her chips when I had won, or at least had been able to stay even with the game? It was so damn unfair. Then and there I decided to push for legalized prostitution to save boys from themselves but mostly to save girls like Susy. Why was it some kids could cope with life and others couldn't? Had I simply lucked out of tragedy because I had dated three different types instead of three Yalies or because, inherently, I was more mature and valedictorian and had more poise and was made of sterner stuff? Or was it because I'd been taking Core Living, which taught you how to live effectively, at the U while no course like it was available to Suse at Michigan State? That was to laugh. My prof for Core Liv was Dr. Sneed, who was known among students as "Slammin' Sam" after the great pro golfer because he was always slamming books down on his desk when his classes ticked him off. He really went ape over Henry David Thoreau. Most profs in the humanities do. They would prefer to live in a sort of world-wide Walden, nothing but isolated woodlots, each with its own shack and pond, in which, being the intelligentsia and keeping journals, they would have status. They refuse to work with the world the way it is. In Core Liv we read excerpts from *Walden;* kids mainly read excerpts in school these days because there isn't time in a ten-week term to plow through the unabridged; and then Dr. Sneed assigned a short theme on the subject "Why I Wish I Had Been Thoreau." This went over like a lead balloon. Nobody in the class wished he had been. Most of the kids, though, faked out their themes with stuff about how neat it would be to poop around nature alone and build their own shacks with their own hands and nonconform and be civilly disobedient and maintain their identity and be buddies with fish and owls and mice and God, etc. I balked. I wrote what I really thought. I was sure Thoreau would have. I don't recall my every monumental idea but here is an abridged version of my theme since you are probably also short of time:

The point I wish to make in this paper is that Thoreau *wasn't*. In my opinion, my generation is the luckiest that ever lived. Historically, we have missed everything draggy. We were too late for hot wars and depressions are things the folks brag about while we bob for cherries in their Manhattans. We have had ample allowances, cars, driver training, luxury schools which never overtaxed our intellects, indulgent parents, and the miracle of television. Our future, too, is great. Jobs are abundant and pay well. We may marry practically when we choose and hence are never frustrated sexually. I have no information concerning Henry David's libido but some winter nights in Massachusetts must have been mighty *icy*.

It is a new thing for a generation to go around feeling fortunate all the time. We have to watch ourselves; we have to be sly; because our only problem is that the world is an *Indian-giver*. It cannot decide whether it wants us to enjoy the fruits of its labors or to be contrite that we have them. Society has a schizoid notion that perhaps it should retrieve what it's given. As a consequence we are shot at and challenged and criticized and deplored and niggled perpetually and from all sides. Teachers and parents and faculty and ministers and newspaper editors have the mission of not leaving us in peace. Spare the Sputnik and spoil the child. We are not grateful enough, responsible enough, ambitious enough, individualistic enough, serious enough. We are silent and delinquent and inscrutable and we don't care a used cigarette filter about world conditions or citizenship or morality or democracy or organized religion. In other words, we are not like *YOU*.

You are damn right, we're not. You did not shape us in your image, you made us what you would have liked to be, and now you are not satisfied. I'm sorry. We *are*. O, we recognize that our experience has been limited; we have never lived in the woods; we have never had to trudge to town; and this first-class, red-carpet, jet-prop flight through youth we regret a little. But the luggage of our discontent weighs less because we have so many other advantages. Our good fortune we accept, thank you. To it we are very well-adjusted. We refuse to rock the boat for the sake of lights and shadows on the water. If it pleases you we will pretend to be what we are not. Punch our buttons and we will produce the right answers.

But I would address myself to the older generation in this manner. We never asked to be so lucky. We did not vote to be born when we were, we were not polled at conception on our environmental preferences. If it gives you a large charge to take out on us your envy, proceed. You cannot hurt us. In our transcendental way we are thoreauly content. We are as remote, as hermetic, as untouchable, really, as a woman eight months along. The world can go to hell in a basket for all she cares. She will have her baby. We will have ours."

8

For example, there are the Zuni Indians of our own Southwest. The admired personality type is one who is moderate in all things, peaceful and restrained. Contrast the Zuni with the Dobu of New Guinea.

CORE LIVING

Jai alai is a game in which two teams of two players heave a hard ball or pelota around a court with high walls by means of wicker baskets on their arms and where Ramona wanted us to go with her was the Fronton Antilles to bet on a particular game. So there we were the next night, Wednesday, the same academic underground, TV and Ramona, who had pulled the cold dodge and got the night off, Basil and Ryder and me, Tuggle and Quentin, betting like crazy on the team of Piston and Arreaga vs. Hannibal and Salsito. I have a lot of trouble with transitions. Tuggle and I had lost a whole day's tan due to being up all night and had left the sack only to dress for the rendezvous with The Scylla of Sex.

This was the deal. Most of the players at the Fronton Antilles were Cuban and so part of the underground and willing to set up an occasional game so that bettors in the know could pull off a real financial coup for the revolution. The catch was, if the big winners were Cuban the management might sniff chicanery, so Ramona's function was to ring in Americans who would be above suspicion to milk the pigeons. We were Americans and darling, innocent college kids to boot. She provided us with $50 each, which we put on the noses of Piston and Arreaga at two-to-one odds. It was very exciting even though a sure thing and we ate hot dogs and drank beer in lieu of dinner and clapped to the organ music and had fun. The players were terrific tragedians. When Piston, for example, a big, handsome, mustached gigolo-type, would flub a point he would throw himself bodily against the screen in front of the gallery and covering his face like The Melancholy Dane beat his head against the wire and we would boo him without pity. They made the game very close and dramatic till the last point, and when Piston and Arreaga triumphed we cheered and waved our bet slips until one of the bet girls came up the aisle to pay us off, at which juncture Ramona cut the Fronton whispering to meet her at the car with the loot. We won $300 over our original investment.

We got the shock at the car. Ramona's interest in the revolution, it seemed, was not entirely disinterested. Beside the Mark XX she was locked in such a carnivorous clinch with a man that her entire face seemed to disappear without a trace in his mustache. We waited clearing our throats until they broke. It was Piston, the jai alai player! She introduced him with great pride and chastity, pronouncing his name Hay-soos Pee-stone, and he shook hands and grinned and could speak scarcely a word of English. We sort of stood around not daring to look at TV Thompson. Tragedy should not be a *spectator* sport and we had witnessed enough of late. I had told her only the night before that he loved her and asked her to let him down gently. Evidently she had decided it would be more merciful to use a pelota. This was it. TV took The Shaft gallantly, shaking hands with Jesus Piston, who called him *"compadre"* but I thought of Susy and the pool.

Then Ramona got galvanic and said we were moving the action to the dog track, so we tore off in the Mark XX to be in time for the last race. Here the deal was slightly different but equally espionage. Arriving in time we went not to the stands but the kennels where the greyhounds were being marched around on leashes barking and looking racy. We waited for the connection. It came. One of the handlers wore a mustache, gestured at his mutt, and Ramona whispered his name was Ubeda II, he was the brother of Ubeda I and his Marimba Band, the race was arranged and this animal, a bitch named Persephone, would come in. This was hard to accept because she looked lethargic and plump enough to have pups but we followed Ramona and Jesus to the $50 window and bought in at four-to-one odds, then headed for the grandstand.

Persephone may have been a dog most nights but in that race she nearly apprehended the bunny. Again we cheered and lined up at the pay window. We had parlayed $50 each into a hemispheric total of $1500, net! Estimating happily in Spanish, Ramona and Jesus figured that would procure five bazooks and five 80-millimeter mortars with appropriate ammunition and maybe a few hand grenades thrown in. On the way to a bar to celebrate we felt so mystic and eleemosynary that we began learning the Cuban national anthem from Jesus and singing it at the tops of our voices.

I cannot recall the name or décor of the bar we went to but I will never forget what happened there. Jesus met the bartender in the men's bique and passed on the handle and we were having a drink and making small anti-Batista talk when TV suddenly tapped for silence with a stirrer and made the following announcement:

"Fellow patriots, I would merely like to say that I have resolved to quit school and sell my car and go at once to Cuba."

It was atomic. Most of us had observed how tied-up and unebullient he had been since the jai alai but we had not dreamed he could be contemplating anything so drastic.

"My God," Ryder said.

"Compadre!" Jesus said.

"My heroo!" Ramona cried.

"No, TV!" Tuggle said.

"Why, Thompson?" Basil demanded.

"Is it because of Latin lovers?" I said.

TV, the good showman, waited until the house was silent again. "Why? I'll tell you. Because it is a far, far better thing that I do, than I have ever done."

Everyone but Ramona and Jesus tried to dissuade him but he was adamant. He ramified by saying that being the Mike Todd of Michigan State no longer satisfied, that subconsciously he had been searching for a cause and this seemed not only to be a solid one but geographically convenient. I knew he was in earnest because I remembered him telling me beside the Bahia-Mar Yacht Basin that what he secretly would most like to be was "some kind of a damn saint." Besides, he said, the selflessness of the Phi Bete from Minnesota still obsessed him; he was bored by the contemporary comedy of manners, he was ready at last, psychologically and spiritually, to play a better class of music on "Thompson's Turntable." He would peddle the Porsche tomorrow and be off. Perhaps he would fight, even die manning one of the very bazookas or mortars we had ourselves earned tonight; perhaps, with his qualifications, he could best serve by getting for the revolution a better press in the U.S.

We listened, we stared at him with mingled horror and admiration. It was sort of a salute to one about to die.

"Sidney Carton," Tuggle breathed.

Ramona removed her harlequins with a kind of rhinestone gravity. She thought TV's deed a "sooperb hooman act." Would he mind, she asked, if she plunged it in the Miami papers after he had gone, and also fed them an item about the boy from Minnesota? He replied no, as well as anyone *alive* he recognized the value of publicity. That was the trouble, she said: even though Cuba was so close, the revolution had never really captured the imagination of the American public because it seemed a purely internal, Cuban matter. What was needed was something like this, the volunteering of an American student for service under liberty's banner. This would make the struggle personal. The martyred name of TV Thompson could be a shining symbol, in case he became a casualty, like those of Schweitzer and Bolívar and Lafayette and Pilsudski. Then she uttered the words that pressed the button:

"I woonder," she mused, "if some other lil coolege boons mightn't be in the mood?"

"Meaning what?" TV said.

"Well, if yoo go it's sweet and all that but if there was a groop it would really be newswoorthy."

"Like, you mean, the Abraham Lincoln Brigade," TV said, "in the Spanish Civil War."

Ramona let him run with the bait. "Of coorse, there'd have to be a recrooting campaign."

"A good time, the end of vacation," TV said to himself, beginning to build. "Give them an alternative to going back to school."

She set the hook. "And somebody with genioos to proomoote it."

Slowly, slowly TV Thompson's six feet four soared above us, borne upward on the thrust of an idea. His hands buzzed our heads. His voice cracked:

"The Lauderdale Legion!"

It hung in the smoke of the bar for a long while before we shot it down with exclamations and protests and comments, etc. But the truth was that there in that unknown bar, on that night, the whole operation was conceived and the machinery set in motion. What bothered me at first was that I thought The Scylla of Sex had *used* TV; that the whole chemistry of his reaction was one of unrequited love; but at last I recognized she was only a catalyst. This was the vastest challenge, in human terms, his entrepreneurial talents had ever faced, a project big enough for a man and idealistic enough for a boy. His operations might at last move off-campus. What had begun with Barbara Hutton could conceivably end in world headlines. Our booth in that bar really became Jackson, The City of Action. So sober and detailed became the intrigue that we switched from drinks to Irish coffee. Ramona and TV did most of the planning and the rest of us responded according to our various natures, personalities, life-goals, etc. Basil and I threw out suggestions. Tuggle and Quent joined in a withdrawn, lovelorn sort of way. Ryder listened but refused to participate. Finally, after about an hour, he stood up and straightened his rep tie.

"Merrit, I'm going," he said. "I'm catching a cab. Are you coming with me?"

"Don't be soobversive!" Ramona spat.

Ryder smiled adultly. "This is the stupidest. As a matter of fact, it's kindergarten. In the first place why should any of these jokers down here volunteer when they'll give blood to evade their own draft? In the second place you lose citizenship by bearing arms for a foreign power. In the third, I came to Florida to relax and decide a few things and if you think I'll screw up the last two days of my vacation for a stunt as Boy Scout and yo-yo as this, you are stark raving. My God, it's worse: it's *Big Ten*. Merrit, are you coming?"

The Club looked at me. I felt history or a nervous breakdown hanging in the balance. I was really torn. I couldn't blame him either. A songwriter and Socrates of jazz, a hotbox coed like Tuggle, an emerged piano man, TV Thompson, an underwater dancer and revolutionary, a jai alai player named Jesus Piston, and Merrit of the U; it was no wonder he could not adapt easily. I was not sure I had.

"Thank you, no, Ryder."

You can imagine what the rejection cost.

So the dice of our youth were cast. After Ryder had gone we really got on the pelota and made arrangements. The recruiting campaign for The Lauderdale Legion would come down the chute the next afternoon. The place, the beach, where else? Ramona would tip off the Miami newspapers and all wire services and Basil would supply men, music, and something martial by way of a singing commercial. TV took on the rest.

We closed the nameless bar and dispersed directly to our sacks, even Tuggle and Quent, agreed we would need all our strength for the morrow. We parted in a state of exhilaration that was practically narcotic.

Dr. Sneed was right and I was wrong, really. Thoreau *was* lucky. Kids today often get so involved in a mad whirl that they have no perspective; but it is only partly their fault. When they want to slow down or seek solitude, society will not let them. In our case Ramona and Jesus and Batista represented society, but even *on* campus, which is supposed to be all ivy and ivory and reclusive, the pace is to the swift. So that students will stay spastic the various U's provide a ratrace called "extracurricular activities" and when they close down for even an instant we loose our own rodents. For example, class, let me rough in a typical winter term week at the U, which may be atypical but will relay the general impression. First, sorority rushing went on all week. Every afternoon two thousand freshman girls girded themselves in hats, high heels and fixed smiles and thronged from house to house and Introductory Tea to Introductory Tea. By Friday afternoon you could cut your preference list to three sororities and skidded to those and then waited for Saturday's mail to see if one of them had condescended to invite you to the Final Tea on Sunday. Second, each night there was also rehearsal for Unirama, the yearly carnival staged in the field house by all campus organizations for charity. Each dorm had a show in its own booth and East Swander's was called "Coolan' Rouge," the theme being a trip to a Paris restaurant complete with Toulouse-Lautrec types and naughty can-can dancers and I was one of the chorus line so each night we rehearsed the can-can for an hour. But also, as if this weren't sufficiently inclusive, third, it was the week of Snow Sculpture, an inter-dorm contest to see which could sculpt the most elaborate thing of snow and ice on the front lawn and win a trophy and I was on the committee for that and had to be out each afternoon with a squad of girls in ten-above-zero temperature packing snow and icing it with a hose. Our design was a giant rocket, pointed heavenward, which was supposed to represent "The Aspirations of Youth." Incidently, there were also classes as usual, of course, and I had two term papers due. By Friday afternoon we had lost two girls on the squad to pneumonia and I was ready to scream stop the world, I want to get off! That night I danced the can-can at Unirama from seven to midnight; we tried to cram in four shows an hour in order to take in more tickets in order to win a trophy for East Swander so that the chorus line, I figured, performed twenty times. It is not how much education you acquire any more, it is how many trophies. It is a lasting thrill to dance the can-can, which is very strenuous, twenty times while boys with bad complexions and horny profs gaze up your crotch.

Saturday. In the mail I had invites to all three Final Teas on Sunday. When I returned, ecstatic, to my room, Dee-Dee, one of my two roommates, had gone into convulsions. Dee-Dee was a snob, frankly, who would have gone to a girls' school instead of the U except that her grades were motley. Her folks were very nouveaux riches. She was thin, insecure, inclined to doing earthy things like electric-razoring her armpits while you tried to study, and personally *non grata* to about everyone in the precinct. But she had received no bids to Final Teas and was threatening to jump from a window or slash her wrists. We called her folks long distance to come and take her home and held her incommunicado till they arrived two hours later. In the interim I was writing a term paper. Then that afternoon the squad went outdoors to finish "The Aspirations of Youth" because the Snow Sculpture judging would be at four o'clock, only to find there had been a thaw. One of the girls let out a little shriek: "Yikes, that's no rocket, it's the world's champion phallus!" She was right. We had to tear the whole damn, lewd thing down before the judges showed and tossed us out of school. That night we got in five shows per hour at Unirama and danced the can-can twenty-five times. When I returned to the dorm I found practical jokers; in other words, nondaters; had been busy. My bed was short-sheeted, my drawers turned upside-down, my soap coated with clear nail polish, and my shower cap filled with toothpaste.

Sunday. I woke feeling weak. I had no appetite. The glands under my chin were swollen. When I dragged out of bed I had a floating sensation. I had heard of these symptoms. I managed to dress and reel on high heels the mile to the first Final Tea, then another mile to the second, then half a mile to the third. I fell down on the ice only once. Somehow I managed to maintain the fixed, brittle smile and keep up my end of the inane conversations, answering and asking questions like "Where are you from?" and "What are you majoring in?" and "Don't you honestly think fraternity men are smoother than GDI's?" But at the last house, Rho Delta Rho, I went berserk. I was sitting amid about six actives all giving me the third-degree about my father's income-bracket in the most snotty, supercilious manner when I suddenly knew I wanted no part of any sorority. So I said, lowering my voice and smiling ingenuously, that since they were about to become my sisters in dear old Rho Delta, la-la-la, they should be willing to help me, I had inadvertently contracted a social disease from some grisly fraternity man and did they know where I might go for treatment? That slaughtered that. I practically crawled back to East Swander. That night I was gradually ebbing in bed and writing the other term paper and eating a peanut-butter-and-banana sandwich and trying to advance the process of education a hair forward when our phone rang and it was my other roomie, Linda, the one who had scooped me on symbiosis, calling to break the news. She had been married that afternoon in Angola, Indiana, and was on her way back to the dorm. The kids in the precinct went crazy with traditional preparations. The tradition at the U, when a girl gets married or engaged or even pinned, is that she must be "tubbed," that is, dunked fully-clad in a bathtub full of cold water and whatever barfy ingredients are available. I should fill you in on Linda before she reaches East Swander. She was a junior and a real brain. She aced all her courses and officered swads of organizations. She was very well-adjusted to everything except boys, who were scared to date her because she was such an intellectual. To compensate she overstarched and had constantly to diet, although otherwise she was quite goodlooks. Of all people, her getting married was the most colossal and unexpected. When she arrived we tubbed her in a soup du jour of coffee grounds, ice water, ink, perfume, detergent, mothballs and cigarette butts and were serenading her with gay hymeneal hymns when she started to cry. It was the most grievous, pitiable sobbing we'd ever heard. It required hours to get the whole synopsis. She had dated this boy only two or three times and today they had gone cruising in his car all day and drinking beer in various locales and got quite snockered and on the spur of the hops he had suggested they tool over to Angola and be married. He was fairly goodlooks and it suddenly seemed to her to be the main chance. She went through with it and immediately misgivings assailed her like a native tribe. He mentioned he had trouble keeping a two-point, or C, average. She was practically Phi Bete. He was not, nor ever would be, her mental equal. She could picture herself on their fortieth anniversary teaching him to read and write. Now he waited outside East Swander in the car for her. She was supposed to pack a bag and go to some friend's beersmelly apartment to have their wedding night. If she did, she would really be married and it could never be annulled. If she didn't, and it was annulled, what if she never had another proposal? Should she be marital at this point or fend him off until they could have a few more dates to see if they were really in love? Either way she would have to inform her folks, who would send her into the storm. How could we advise her? The U was a marriage mart; parents knew that when they sent us; but during a sale you can't take things home on approval. She sat there in the barfy tub, teeth chattering, combing cigarette butts and melting mothballs out of her hair with her hands, wailing, begging for advice, crying as though for her departed girlhood.

Monday. We checked at the Registrar's Office and he *did* have a C average and that was the day I went to the mat with Dr. Raunch over "random dating" and disappeared into the deanmill and then three days later into the Health Service with advanced mono.

I waited on the beach. The weather had warmed again and the sky was cobalt blue. It was three o'clock and that was scheduled to be destiny's hour but there was no sign. The thousands of kids, the future of America, seemed to be functioning normally; playing bridge, talking, listening to portables, etc.; but they were less languorous, they seemed to be more *motivated*. You knew they were toiling harder on their tans. You knew they were planning parties to end all parties. You knew *they* knew they had only this day of vacation and the next. It was sort of uncanny to go up on my elbows and look out upon the brown hordes and realize that they, too, had clustered into nuclei like ours, had fallen in and out of love, had gone round and round with their own problems, had engaged in myriad adventures. It would have been kicks to be omniscient and be able to tell how they had made out in Florida, who had won and lost, what would happen to them, etc. Not far away was a lifeguard platform with a guard on it yawning and scratching his development. Then I spotted Ramona and Jesus Piston standing beneath it and around them some men with press cameras and some other men who must have been reporters because they did not look like reporters. That wasn't all. Sitting their Martian motorcycles were two imported policemen, also waiting. One of them I recognized as Ahbedam. That wasn't all. In a parked car, keeping the beach under surveillance, were three men in white shirts and innocuous ties and Hawkshaw expressions who had to be FBI agents. I came to my feet with the drama.

Someone touched my arm.

"I'm sorry about last night, Merrit," Ryder said. "I really am."

"Hark!"

For I heard the sound, distant, a hot tenor sax, a song on the salt air, inspiriting, the dialectic rattle of a drum. The historic march up the beach had begun! I went to tiptoe. A commotion among the kids. Here they came! This was the order of march: Three boys abreast, striding erect in swim trunks, with heads bandaged like The Spirit of Seventy-Six, Basil in the center carrying the flag of the República de Cuba, on one side Archie blowing his wild Mulligan tenor, on the other Ray, beating a jazz summons on a snare.

Then Quentin and some boys carrying big signs:

SPEND SPRING TERM IN CUBA!
REMEMBER THE MAINE!
SIC SEMPER TYRANNIS!
OUR MINDS ARE MADE UP DON'T CONFUSE US WITH FACTS!
LET'S BOMB BATISTA!
ENROLL IN REVOLUTION 202!
GARCIA, WE GET YOUR MESSAGE!
SEEK YOUR IDENTITY IN ORIENTE!
JOIN THE LAUDERDALE LEGION!

Then Tuggle and some auxiliary girls passing out mimeographed words to the war song Basil had written and a coil of kids singing it to the sax and the progressive drum:

"Our generation's beat!
You repeat.
We answer, We're the most!
That's no boast.

So to hell with your attacks—
We got a red-hot tenor sax—
And The Spirit of Fifty-Eight is GREAT!

You prophesy our doom,
In your gloom.
You try to tranquilize us
From the womb.
But despair is for the birds—
We will make you eat your words—
For The Spirit of Fifty-Eight is GREAT!

Please ignore—
Our capers and our japes—
Find us a revolution
And we'll fight like apes!

So stick your apprehension
In your ear.
Your preaching and your tension
And your fear.
Radioactive we may be—
But we're mad for liberty!

Our forebears got their kicks—
From The Spirit of Seventy-Six—

But The Spirit of Fifty-Eight is GREAT!"

I was clutched. The effect was simply *supreme*. And that, or Archie's tenor, or Tuggle's figure, or the total impact of the parade, or curiosity or something, pulled at least three hundred kids along, possibly more. In fact, by the time everything ground to a halt before the lifeguard platform and the last blast of sax and roll of drum died there was a real multitude. Suddenly TV Thompson spidered up the ladder to the platform and cheers for his appearance rent the heavens. Stripped to the waist, around which he had buckled a big Wyatt Earp pistol and cartridge belt, his bony, burned, peeling breast expanded to its fullest, he wore an ancient World War I doughboy helmet lettered Château-Thierry and tipped jauntily to one side. He bowed and held up his endless arms.

"Thanks, group!" he cried. "Thanks a lot. I know it was a great sacrifice for you to come out here today."

Cheers.

"These are the times that try men's souls!"

Cheers.

"Seriously. The pitch should be obvious to you. We've had a ball down here, all of us, but they're about to lower the boom of time on us. It's back to the ratrace. But I clue you in, you guys can have that slush. As for me, give me sun or give me death!"

Cheers.

"So that's why this meeting. I won't give you any hard sell. This revolution in Cuba may turn out to be rancid but it's the only one available. And let's face it, Batista is the bottom of the human barrel. Now a couple hundred of us could go over there and soak up more sun and some frozen daiquiris and clean up the whole Caribbean in a couple of weeks. How they going to keep us down on the campus after we've seen Havana? I mean, you want to live forever?"

Cheers.

"Seriously. You know how futile you feel. What can I do about Russia, you say. Or Africa? Will they hear me in the United Nations? Hell, no. How much drag do I have with Lyndon Johnson? But none. You can't even write your Congressman unless you're twenty-one and at the summit they're too senile for our age-level. It's like we're little kids standing at the exit of the world's biggest supermarket trying to open the door for people coming out laden down with groceries. Whenever we get ready to help the damn door flies open on some damn electric-eye principle and there we stand feeling stupid. It's frustrating. But this is one thing we *can* do. It won't take much time or cash and the best thing is, it doesn't have to be a *production*. We can do it *casually*. If I could have a couple hundred of your names and local phone numbers this afternoon I could overnight arrange for transportation and contact you tomorrow and the expeditionary force could take off by next day. It would be real simple. And it would be a good thing. We could have something to leave our kids besides some shares of General Motors. I feel that any guy who chickens out on an easy, part-time operation like this is a nurd. In fact, he's a *green* nurd. Put it this way: somewhere the sun is shining, somewhere the people shout, but let's not have the country say of us, *this* generation has struck out. How about it, group? We will fight them on the beaches, we will fight them in the casinos, and in years to come men will say of us, this was their *hottest* hour! So all volunteers for The Lauderdale Legion, forward! Fire when ready, Gridleys! Every man a general, no close-order drill, no officers by Act of Congress, bring your own stationery and Bibles and clean sox! C'mon, men, live it up with The Lauderdale Legion!"

Nothing. Absolutely nothing. Unbelieving, TV waited a full, nauseating minute.

"Sign up and see the world!"

He took off his shell-rims.

"Well?"

His mouth opened and closed.

"Well?"

Then at the rear of the throng, raucous and derisive, the voices rose in song:

" 'Collegiate, collegiate, yes, we are collegiate!' "

It was The Nassoons, the chorus from Princeton. It was the worst insult they could have hurled, the lowest blow life could have delivered. Far more effectively than the police or FBI, it broke the kids up. The assembled hundreds died laughing. Slapping their thighs, bending double, they began to disperse, some returning to the sands, many heading merrily for The Sheikh's or the Sand Crab. Down came the signs. The flag of Cuba fell. O, God, God, God, it was horrible! It was more calamitous, more tragic, really, than Susy in the pool. That was physical, this was spiritual. My eyes were so awash with tears I could scarcely make Herbert TV Thompson out. He stood alone on the platform except for the lifeguard yawning and scratching, alone and wilted, the expression on his face that of a little boy caught in a carwash by the truant officers. The Mike Todd of Michigan State had folded out of town.

9

Many collegians admit to a wish to change their personalities during their college years. Concentration, cultural interest, perseverance, leadership and personal charm are the goals most frequently specified by students.

CORE LIVING

It may be bad art to dispel the atmosphere of doom right after the botch on the beach, the collapse of the cause, the utter debacle, but I promised earlier to discuss large families and propose to unleash a few choice words on the subject here. Besides, it is always darkest before The Sheikh's. In my opinion, the present-day preference for quantity over quality is the weediest trend in a long time. Most of the girls I know when asked how many kids they intend to roe assume a Mona Lisa, broodmare look and simper five or six. They admit they have no reason; they just *want* them the way they might *want* five or six lemon Cokes or *want* five or six Fats Domino records. You can't argue it dispassionately because someone is always certain to say smugly it's against her religion to limit conception. People will rationalize *anything*. A scrabble of offspring is part of our standard of living. It doesn't matter a squat if you can afford it, concentrate on it, discipline it, love it, build enough schools and parking space and mental institutions for it. The thing is, copulate and populate. America's conscience now has a credit card. What are we trying to prove by our national birth rate? We cannot whip China and India in the race, nor can we, no matter how we huff and puff in the dark of night, how we zip in and out of delivery rooms, compete with rabbits. We are already short of area in the U.S., already so crowded that we have to *meter* everything. Soon cemeteries will have meters and if the bereaved do not shell out systematically and on the hour they will impound the remains. But what really burns me is that I suspect the whole frenzied contest to outspawn each other is based on pure *ego*. I would like to inquire of every happy, fertile, idiot couple: what in holy hell do you have in your bloodline or heredity or personality that you believe is so damn *special* that you have to endow the earth with it as lavishly as you can, huh? O, I get so damn ticked off and I should not digress just when this book is beginning to develop a little *pace*.

We drank dinner at The Sheikh's and then shambled back to the Shalimar. We did not see Ramona or Jesus Piston who had, like the Arabs, folded and stolen away. We sat around with the body. Florida had caught up with us. We were flaked out from no-food and no-sleep. Tuggle and Quent had their grand passion still but the flame burned low. The conversation was desultory. Someone would say something and it would lie there and expire. The most important thing we could not with decency talk about. It was as though TV had put himself through his own Testing Service and flunked. But so had we, for we had voluntarily, except for Ryder, associated ourselves with this cause. The afternoon had been the all-time fall-through. We had been spurned by our own peer-group.

Finally I felt, since it was half my apartment, that I should give socializing the old college initiative.

ME: Well, it's almost over. Tonight and tomorrow and tomorrow night and that's it. It's been quite great, though, huh?

TV: Great.

BASIL: Great.

RYDER: Great.

TUGGLE: Great.

QUENT: Great.

ME: I still haven't decided what major to declare. I still will not be an Uncom. What should I do?

BASIL: See the chaplain.

RYDER: I have my own problem.

TV: Get some counseling.

TUGGLE: Don't go into teaching. It's a drag.

ME: Well, there's one thing nobody's mentioned down here. I suppose we ought to bring up The Bomb.

RYDER:

TV:

BASIL:

TUGGLE:

QUENT:

ME: I know, how about the Beat Generation?

TUGGLE: What's that?

TV: Never heard of it.

RYDER: I draw a near-blank.

QUENT: They were then.

BASIL: I think they're some guys living in California growing beards. They make a living at it.

TUGGLE: O.

RYDER: I heard there are some in New York, too.

BASIL: There's something about poetry. And coffee.

TV: O.

ME: Well, it's almost over. It's been great, though.

TV: Great.

BASIL: Great.

RYDER: Great.

TUGGLE: Great.

QUENT: Great.

ME: I just thought of something. You know, the six of us are really a unique sect. I bet we have a secret we've had to hide for years. Let's break down. I'll go first. In high school I was valedictorian. My IQ's 134. Tuggle?

TUGGLE: Mer, how could you?

ME: If you don't tell I will.

TUGGLE: Damn. Well, 132.

ME: Basil?

BASIL: 140 something.

ME: Anything over 130 is gifted. I read that somewhere. The top ten per cent. TV?

TV: Who cares?

ME: I do. What grades do you pull?

TV: *C'est la guerre*. I guess almost a four-point.

ME: Practically all-A. Quent?

BASIL: He won't say but I know. They told me once, at school. Somewhere over 150, which is in the genius range.

TUGGLE: Quent, darling, we're eugenic!

ME: Ryder?

RYDER: I take the Fifth. A gentleman would.

BASIL: My uncouth butt.

ME: I know you have to hold yourself down to keep a B average. You told me.

RYDER: Damn. As a matter of fact, 138.

ME: And there we are.

BASIL: My God, we're all brains.

TUGGLE: Ssssssh.

QUENT: Pianissimo.

TV: Then how did we foul out this afternoon? All that promotion and not one sign-up.

RYDER: It was too public. Who wants his picture in the papers being gung-ho? Besides, it was a one-man show. What you need today is teamwork.

BASIL: No drama.

TUGGLE: We tried. We're not responsible.

ME: Yes, we are, we're in the top ten of our generation. We're supposed to lead, now and later. This afternoon was symbolic. If we flub something small, how can we ever swing anything big?

BASIL: How nauseating can you get?

RYDER: Just because you're literate doesn't mean you have to eat python meat.

TV: She's got a point, though. Society has a large investment in us. We're responsible to something, I'm not sure what.

BASIL: You're responsible to yourself. If that happens to coincide, fine. If not, tough.

ME: No one's being honest. I think we all feel fungous about this afternoon but we would cut out our tongues before we'd admit it. We *did* strike out. And the cause *isn't* Mickey Mouse. *We* are.

TV: Thanks.

BASIL: Thanks.

RYDER: Thanks.

TUGGLE: Thanks.

QUENT: *Gracias.*

After this dialogue all attempts at artificial respiration on the evening failed. Tuggle and Quent eventually bowed. That left Ryder, Basil, TV and me sitting around using up the oxygen. Suddenly I realized. There I was with three boys; three, I re-counted; all of them interesting and potential. This had never happened to me before. This was partly what girls came to Florida for. To look at them in turn, to recall that I had made mad, mad love with each of them, was to feel slightly alley-catish. Thank goodness and virtue that was over. Safety lay, obviously, in numbers, and the addition of talent had enabled me for days to be as sexless as Aunt Sal.

Suddenly I caught on to something else. They were not going! Each was determined to wait until the other two had decamped. It was to be a battle of wills, with Merrit of the U between the lines.

Basil lit a cigar.

TV slumped deep in defeat.

Ryder whistled Brown's Fight Song or something between his teeth.

It was the ultimate human impasse. After about an hour it became unbearable.

"Does anyone," I said brightly, "have any ideas about the reunification of Germany?"

It was Ryder who cracked.

"Look, rustics, I'd like five minutes alone with Merrit."

"Next," said TV.

"Next," said Basil.

"I am not," I said, "a barbershop."

They glowered.

"You two mind," Ryder said, "waiting outside?"

Basil and TV strolled out onto the veranda synchronizing their watches.

The moment we were alone Ryder said he had reached one of the two decisions it was necessary for him to make.

He said he knew now, absolutely, that he loved me with all his heart.

He asked me if I would sleep with him tonight.

I said no, that love seemed to be little more than a tourist attraction in Lauderdale.

But, he protested, I had told him I loved him. Had saying it meant nothing to me?

He was so handsome, in an F. Scott Fitz way, that he would be handsome even before breakfast.

Yes, I said, I had been sincere. But I was afraid that, with less than two days left, it would be in and out of the hay and back to Brown and inform the boys that what they had heard about Midwest coeds was true. See what had happened to Susy.

No, he said fervently, no, as a matter of fact he loved me with all his heart.

O, I said.

Would I, then, he breathed in my ear, sleep with him tomorrow night, our last? We would have his uncle's house entirely to ourselves. It would be a preview of marriage.

Enter TV.

Exeunt Ryder.

TV said all was now revealed to him. I was the only girl he had ever known who could minister to his split-personality. He loved me violently and wanted me to wife.

I said I was touched and grateful but it was only rebound from Ramona.

He said no, that had been highschool of him but it was entirely finis. He had matured, I was really the one, and would I be with him again tonight beside the Bahia-Mar Yacht Basin?

No, I said.

But I had assured him I could love him, he protested. Had I been handing him a line?

No, I said, I had been sincere.

Then, he said, this day had been dire enough, was I to crush him completely? Was he to receive at my hands the same treatment he had received from the sorority queen at Michigan State? Would I not be with him tomorrow night, our last?

He still wore about his skinny waist the Wyatt Earp pistol and cartridge belt.

I said I did not know.

One thing, he said emotionally, one boon I was obligated to grant. Since tomorrow night was the last, there should be a party to end all parties, and the perfect site would be Ryder's uncle's house. Would I arrange to be there, so that he and a few friends could be assured of access?

I asked why.

Because babyroo, he whispered, because you are *responsible*.

Enter Basil.

Exeunt TV.

Burning his cigar to a fiery brand, Basil said that he had faced it at last, jazz was not enough in life for him, nor was his flock, I was truly his big girl, his Penelope among the wooers, to whom he must come home.

In other words, he said, running a hand along a silvery temple, he loved me.

O, I said.

Moreover, he said, he was proud to ask me to marry him. He had the means for matrimony and if I would say yes we could be wed immediately, return together to Ohio State, to which I could transfer my credits from the U, and eventually have a deferred honeymoon when The Quartet went to San Francisco, where he hoped they might make their debut at The Jazz Workshop.

In the meantime, he added, after what we had wrought together within its walls, this apartment would always be to him The Love Workshop. Might we not reopen it tonight?

No, I said.

Tomorrow night, then, our last?

I said I did not know.

Was I, he demanded, in love with that Leaguer?

I said I did not know that either.

I must not be, he asserted. He had that morning dashed off a Strauss-type waltz which would better express the dialectic of his ideas. He would do it for me and leave me to mull and repeat his proposal tomorrow. He banged out the door.

I collapsed over a chair.

Of the three, all of whom had declared they loved me eternally, etc., only Ryder had *not* asked me to marry him.

Basil returned, carrying his bass like a cave woman, tearing at the canvas, tuned up, paused, then played:

"Don't marry an Organization Man,
 Or after you are wed:
 Though he's talented and witty—

He'll adore you by committee!
Marry *me*,
Instead.

Don't marry an Organization Man,
Don't swear to share his bed:
His caresses in the PM—
Will be computed by IBM!
Marry *me*,
Instead.

In communication
He may be well-grounded;
His personality
May be well-rounded;
In Connecticut
He may be well-connected—
But do you want a husband
Other-directed?

Don't marry an Organization Man,
No, indeed, you must lead, not be led:
For when he should be havin' you—
He'll make love to Madison Avenue!
Don't conform
To the norm—
Or submerge
In the urge—
But instead, marry *me*,
Keep your individuality!
Marry *me!*
Marry *me!*
Marry *me!*"

10

If your hypotheses are not consistent with your observations, you must either change or modify your original beliefs or reject or question the observations. This procedure is the essence of learning and discovery. Obtain a frog from your instructor. Determine its sex.

CORE SCIENCE

March 30, 1958, the last day of spring vacation, the day before twenty thousand kids would tool north and leave

Lauderdale to the older generation for another year, a very unknown day. Mainly it was occupied by putting final touches on your tan, reassembling your gear so it could be thrown in a suitcase in minutes, and making contact with your ride home to find out the time of departure. Most kids planned to be up all night at parties to end all parties and then take off about dawn and drive fifteen hundred miles straight through.

These things I did, too. Tuggle was gone most of the day somewhere with Quent. I did not see or hear from Basil. Around noon Ryder phoned. Could he pick me up about eight? I hesitated. This was it. He loved me more than ever, he pleaded, and he had great news. All right, I said. An hour later TV phoned. Would I be at Ryder's uncle's house that night? I said yes I would be and no I would not. TV began the hard sell. I waited and then asked why, what was the object? He was evasive again, saying all he wanted was a yes or no, to which I replied no, then, no, no, and hung up.

I sat in the sun by the pool at the Shalimar trying to attain Nirvana and not think. But I could not overcome a sense of *impending*. It was as though I had tied myself to something weighty, given it a shove, and was about to be pulled more irrevocably than ever before into the pool of life.

The mansion on Chula Vista Drive was even more fabulous, if possible, by night. Ryder flicked on swads of switches to show how the palm trees and pool and even the *Ataxia II* moored down at the dock on the canal could be illuminated. But in a little while, of course, he had made us a highball and we were in the master bedroom with the drapes drawn and ourselves sort of draped along a swish divan necking in an hors d'oeuvres way. Besides his white bucks and ivy-striped sport shirt Ryder wore round his neck an ascot scarf; one of my teen-age ambitions, based on men in movies, had been to date a boy suave enough to wear an ascot scarf.

"Merrit, darling, ask you now to marry me I can," he breathed, fouling up his syntax with kisses.

"Why now?" I breathed.

"Because I've decided." From his shirt pocket he took several sheets of papers covered with figures and began explaining them. He had spent two days figuring out what his retirement income would be, as an executive, from the three companies which had offered him jobs upon graduation. The home laundry manufacturer projected highest at age sixty-five, twelve thousand yearly. He had sent them a telegram of acceptance this morning.

"That means, darling, that we can be engaged anytime and married in June." He knelt on the floor beside me and took my hands. "Merrit, I have the honor to ask you to be my wife."

"But what about Couplequip?" I asked.

"I'd have practically no income for a year or two. We'd have to wait."

"I wouldn't mind," I said. "I know it's out to lunch for a girl to be willing to wait five minutes these days but I am, for the sake of your independence and happiness and things."

"It's too chancy, darling."

"If you can't take risks now, Ryder, when can you?"

"We've been over that ground."

"These are our life signals. We should get them straight."

"Mine are." He stood up angrily. "You're living in the wrong decade, Merrit. I'm sorry to disillusion you but my school is Brown, not Princeton, and you are no Zelda. As a matter of fact, you're living in the wrong century."

I stood up just as angrily. "As a matter of your own damn fact, Ryder Smith, don't you see that I'm only trying to keep you from becoming an ulcerman?"

"Fundamentally," he said, "fundamentally you have no problem because you *are* an Uncom."

That stung me to the intellectual quick. "You don't want love, you want utility! You don't want a wife, you want a station wagon! Sturdy, serviceable, good mileage, capable of carrying about four kids but still glamorous enough to drive to parties at night! Well, I love you, Ryder, yes, but I refuse to marry a razor-blader!"

"What in hell is that?"

"A razor-blader is a man who won't put his used blades in the used-blade slot in the medicine cabinet because he isn't sure how deep it is and worries he will fill up the basement or something of his house!"

"Well, my God." He took a huge gulp of his highball. "My God."

"Ryder," I said, "in your opinion what is the most important thing a person has?"

"His personality."

"Okay, and how do you define personality?"
"You and your damn metaphysical questions. Okay, it's the impression you make on other people."
"Aha!" I cried. "I thought so! Then all you are is an impression in other people's minds! Then when you're alone you're nothing, you don't register so you don't even exist!"
"Who wants to be alone?" he shouted.
"It happens to be man's essential condition!" I shouted.
"My aching God," he said, shaking his head. "You really *are* Big Ten. I bet you even listen to Dwight Fiske records."
"And you're really League," I said sadly. "Volleyball in the Colosseum."
We stared at each other across the gulf with all possible gravity and regret.
"You're *young,* Meritt," he said.
"Ryder, you're *old,"* I said.
The doorbell tolled about ten minutes before we heard it.
"Let it go."
"You'd better see."
"Let it go."
"It might be," I said, betraying him not with sarcasm, not with a kiss, but mournfully, "your washer and drier future."
So he opened the door and it was TV Thompson, of course, with a few friends from Pitt and a few from Wesleyan and Amherst and some girls from Denison and each boy balancing on his shoulder a case of cold beer and though Ryder was furious and shouted he would permit no count in his uncle's house they pushed past him and stacked the cases in the living room and started to debate the issue when The Basil Demetomos Quartet arrived with all their instruments and set up in the living room and teed off with "Keep Britain Tidy." It was imperative they buckle down to work again, Basil told me; it had been about three days since they had done any research and they had a lot of records and derivations to get out of their systems.
Ryder cornered me and accused me of plotting the whole thing with TV and demanded I get rid of all these damn kids or he would call thc police, whereupon I warned him about poor *personal relations.*
A veritable horde of youthful humanity was now funneling through the front door. TV had really spread the

word. There were delegations from Michigan, Colgate, Indiana, Penn, Ohio Wesleyan, Syracuse, Dayton and Chicago, etc. The kitchen was stacked to the ceiling with beer cases. No one could afford liquor by this late date and some kids swore they had spent all their going-home-gasoline money for beer and hadn't the foggiest how they would get home and couldn't care less. It was going to be the blast to end all blasts, that was certain, so I helped myself to a beer and prepared to plunge into the maelstrom when who should make an entrance but Ramona, The Scylla of Sex, ecdysiastic in an ice-blue sheath dress and Jesus Piston, his teeth flashing. Ramona told me TV had invited them and promised big things and so her chest "coold" had worsened and she had taken another night off from the San Remo and Jesus had faked a charley-horse or something and been scratched for the evening at the Fronton Antilles.

Someone turned on the lawn lights and pool lights and there were shouts of gay delight about the pool and ooh's and ah's at the sleek beauty of the *Ataxia II* moored at the dock and one gang of kids decided to have beer on the boat and another to go swimming.

There was a phenomenon in the living room: The Quartet kept starting a number and stopping in the middle and starting a new one. I located Tuggle drinking beer and she said Quent had told her they were sort of disintegrating.

I talked a minute with TV, who was eating potato chips and oddly withdrawn. But what really set off the alarm in me was that he was dressed, for the first time in Florida, *standardly*, no eccentric hats or props of any kind.

More kids continued to arrive, sundry battalions from Purdue, Franklin and Marshall, Northwestern, Oberlin, Virginia and MIT. But the prize surprise was the show-up, almost simultaneously, of Ubeda I and his Marimba Band and The Nassoons from Princeton. Ooby, as he was y-clept, set up near the pool and began to beat out the "Castro Cha-Cha-Cha" and other Afro-Cuban rhythms while The Nassoons, who were already bombed, harmonized sweetly on "Tune ev'ry heart and ev'ry voice, bid ev'ry care withdraw."

By now, which was getting on to midnight, if you had put a seismograph near the house that Couplequip had built on Chula Vista Drive the machine would have alerted scientists on the Kamchatka Peninsula. The boy from Jackson, The City of Action, had, without really trying, promoted himself a real bacchanal.

In the pool two teams were putting on a water polo game using a beer can.

I confess with some shame that all the bedrooms were *engagé* as certain couples, about to be riven by spring term, sought privacy to pledge love everlasting.

Wandering about the place I ran into many old friends. There was the boy from Kent State, for example, expounding his theories on how to defeat the Russians to a cell hidden behind beer cases in the kitchen.

I found the girl with raffia hair and cigarette-shaped fingers from Goosecroft urping in a flowerbed.

The Scylla of Sex was persuaded to do her underwater act in the pool, drawing an immense throng not so much by virtue of her grace and lung-power as by the fact that her costume consisted of pants and bra.

Some celibate, antisocial boys from Duke had a poker game going on the flying bridge of the *Ataxia II*.

Every time I saw Jesus Piston he shouted *"Olé!"*

Over a Budweiser I met Basil who informed me The Quartet had gone to hell. Florida had finished the flock. Archie was more Mulligan than ever, Ray more Mel Roach, and Quent, of course, had been raped. But he was in no pain, he loved me, would I marry him and leave with him for Columbus at eight in the morning?

By three A.M. what had been merely Babylonian had become a madathon.

Those two damn boys from Illinois, the diving exhibitionists, had tried to shinny up a palm in order to dive into the pool and fallen instead into some oleanders, spraining arms and legs, etc.

Darting madly about on the lawn was a girl from Bennington playing tennis with an imaginary opponent and a stringless racket.

The Nassoons were singing "The orange moon of flaming hue soars up to cross the Stygian sky" when some boys from Michigan interrupted with "Hail, hail to Michigan, The Champions of the West" and a real melee erupted, resulting in bloody noses, black eyes, broken glasses, etc.

Two fiendish biology majors from Penn staggered in with a Galápagos sea turtle weighing about two hundred pounds which they had stolen somewhere and put in the pool where it fluked wildly about among the beer cans and the resumed water polo game.

I had just commenced to have a terrific count-down feeling about everything when I heard a strange hoarse shout on the lawn which sloped down to the canal. I tooled outside.

It was TV. He was sober, not stoned, but clutched.

"I am going to Cuba!" he shouted. "Now!" He raised an arm, pointing. "I am going in that boat!"

What a hush.

"The hell you are!"

Ryder sprinted from the house, his fists clenched. They faced each other. Ubeda I's Marimba Band ceased playing. So did The Quartet. Kids came down from the pool, silent and dripping. Couples left bedrooms in the mansion and drew near, disheveled. The poker game ended in mid-pot and the Duke boys climbed the lawn. A circle formed about TV and Ryder. I saw Basil and Quent and Tuggle and Ryder. In the floodlights the faces were fascinated and morbid and pastel. It was a mystic moment.

"Thompson, the hell you are," Ryder repeated. "I've had about enough of this collegiate crap. That is a fifty-five thousand dollar Chris-Craft. It doesn't belong to me or even to my uncle. As a matter of fact it belongs to his company, Couplequip, in South Nuxton, Mass. And the whole damn island of Cuba can sink without a trace before I let you lay hand one on it!"

"Tax-dodge, hey?"

It was Basil, advancing pugilistically. "Listen, Smith, let's have a little dialectic. You say this boat belongs to some company, right?"

"That's what I said."

"And that company is a representative American industry, right?"

"So?"

"And American industry is always sounding off about having stake in freedom and free enterprise, right?"

"So?"

"So that company will be goddam glad to get a chance from us to contribute to the cause of freedom—right?"

Cheers from the kids. For an instant Ryder had no reply. Then he tore off his ascot scarf, raised his fists again.

"It's robbery! No, it's grand theft! No, by God, it's worse—it's anarchy!"

Cheers for anarchy from the kids. Basil began to bob and weave, Ryder to circle, getting inadvertently between Basil and TV.

"You bass player!" he cried.

"You selfish buckle-back bastard!" Basil snarled, and suddenly let go with a tremendous, crashing right cross.

He hit TV! Ryder sidestepped and Basil clobbered TV right in the solar plexus! Poor TV sagged, nearly broken in two, all the accumulated wind of his twenty years expelled from him.

Much confusion and fanning and when I could next glimpse Ryder, always the gentleman, he was shaking hands with *both* TV and Basil and I heard him say to TV, "But you can't even find your way out of the channels."

"I can try," said TV stoutly.

"The Coast Guard will stop you before you get a block out to sea."

"Let them."

"Suppose you do make it." Ryder fired his last salvo. "Suppose you get to Cuba. You won't even know where to land."

"I can find out."

"How?"

TV punched him in the shoulder. "The boat's got a phone, man! I'll call up Santiago and say hey, where's the action?"

Amid the laughter Ryder grinned, threw up his hands and faced the ultimate:

"I give up. Take her!"

Yikes, what cheers then!

TV next announced that this would be no production, he was just cutting the academic scene for a while, that was all, and if anyone else wanted to go they were welcome but he was making no pitch, all those who desired transportation could join him on the dock. So saying, he marched down the lawn.

There was much murmuring and milling. Then, and here was the bomb, who else should go marching after TV but Ryder himself, Basil, Quent, Archie, Ray, the trumpet man and the bongo drummer from Ubeda I's band, and all fourteen of The Nassoons!

The hundred or more of us stood aghast, as though at an epiphany, then moved down toward the boat, Ramona teetering ahead on spike heels. She cried out to wait, it was "footile" to take a boat to Cuba empty and wouldn't they delay a few minutes till the underground could bring a cargo desperately needed by the revolution?

TV said they would wait and Jesus ran up to the house to telephone.

The half-hour wait was busy, busy. Ryder, it seemed, did not even know how to operate the boat, but two skippers turned up, one of The Nassoons whose folks, he claimed, had a similar craft at the Minnetonka Yacht Club on the North Shore, wherever that was, and Pablito, the bongo drummer, who spoke no English but had cut bait on a tourist fishing tub and was hence presumed able to navigate. They agreed to share command. The boat was fully gassed, it was found, but there was no food aboard, so a detachment requisitioned all that could be scrounged from the house, a really rugged assortment of such field rations as smoked oysters, miniature sausages, martini olives, and several tins of caviar. Ooby, Jesus, Ramona, TV, Ryder and the two skippers conferred on tactics and decided to try for a debarkation the following night along the northeast coast not far from Guantánamo, which was rebel territory. If Marines from the U.S. Naval Base there resisted the landing, they would be slaughtered to the last man. Then someone commented that *Ataxia II* was a fungous name for a frail bark about to become world-renowned and suggestions were called for.

"Academe!"

"The Golden Fluff!"

"Fidelismo!"

"Mickey Mouse!"

"Titoonic!"

"The Green Nurd!"

This last was perfect, so some kids located paint and a brush in the triple-garage, *Ataxia II* was obliterated and replaced by *The Green Nurd* on the stern and a can of beer poured over the bow in lieu of champagne.

At this point, for security's sake, every light inside and outside the house was doused because the cargo was in process of coming. A whole series of laundry trucks, grocery trucks, panel trucks, etc. began backing into the garage, each of them manned by two men, both mustached. A line of boys was formed down the lawn and onto *The Green Nurd* and countless cases of rifles, machine guns, grenades, bazookas, carbines, mortars and ammunition were passed from hand to hand. So many tons of war matériel were put aboard that there was no room for anyone to go below and *The Green Nurd* sat very low in the water.

If there is anything kids today would rather die than be

it is *flashy*. So I do not know how to describe the tragicomic events of the next few minutes. Words like epic and gallant and selfless are so sterling that a writer can use them only once and I already have about ten times. The trouble is, older, critic-type readers will be bitter if I joke around here, but if I'm serious all my own friends who read the book will hoot. Consequently, to try to satisfy both I guess I will have a crack at the mock-heroic.

March 31, 1958. Fort Lauderdale, Florida. A mansion on Chula Vista girt with lawns and palms. By the tropic dawn's early light you may see a streamlined white-and-mahogany cruiser lying at dock along a blue canal. At her rails striplings stand expectant, about her are grouped a hundred young people, their faces drawn and pale from the night's exertions, the looks upon them a mingling of dedication and disbelief. For it does seem unreal, a dream way far out. Until this morn it has been a game, a quest for love, for laughs, for sun, for respite, a hunt for the iguana of youth which forever impels, forever eludes, and only age makes captive. Now stillness, an instant to reflect that The Lauderdale Legion has after all been mustered, an epic expedition will presently set forth down the canal, out the channel, and a generation's flower will be given to an ocean's discipline, a revolution's vagaries, the horrors of Mars!

The time of parting nighs. A maiden sobs. It is Tuggle. She refuses to allow Quentin to go unless she may accompany him, she cannot live her life alone as an El Ed teacher. Ramona shrugs why not? Castro's bands count many young women among their ranks; they roll bandages, nurse the wounded; a Girls' Auxiliary will get even bigger headlines in the U.S. With a cry of joy Barbara Tuggle leaps aboard, takes shelter in Quent's froggy arms. A girl from Ohio Wesleyan springs to the embrace of a boy from Colgate. The two divers from Illinois hobble up to swell the crew, then three boys from Purdue, then the Russian expert from Kent State. The girl from Bennington takes her solitary stand near the stern. Onward, ever onward, seraphic and tearful, proudly they stream. Impulse glorious, madness divine! The decks by now are jammed. It is time to cast off, to set sail, to voyage far. Through misted eyes I strain to find those dear to me; Ryder, Basil, TV; can there be room for yet another, for Merrit of the U? With heart bursting in my bosom I extend my arms and welcoming gestures, glad cries, receive me.

H-hour! There is much spasticism upon the flying bridge until the two skippers find the ignition and starter buttons. The twin Diesel engines spring to life, the twin exhausts roar and purl upon the waters, the echoes slap from pile-lined shore to shore of the canal! Again the mood alters. Near the bow Basil takes his bass, Archie his tenor, Ray his snare, they are augmented by Ooby's trumpet man, and as they play the kids on land begin to sing the now-immortal words:

"Please ignore—
Our capers and our japes—
Find us a revolution
And we'll fight like apes!

So stick your apprehension
In your ear.
Your preaching and your tension
And your fear.
Our forebears got their kicks—
From The Spirit of Seventy-Six—
But The Spirit of Fifty-Eight is GREAT!"

Weapons are broken out and distributed. I am passed a submachine gun, which I sling over my shoulder girl-guerrilla style.

Massed, The Nassoons increase the din: *"Integer vitae scelerisque purus!"*

"Cast off the lines!"

"Gaff the top-gallants!"

"Unfurl the flags!"

"Start that saga!"

"Bon voyage, buddyroos!"

"Cheers!"

O God, God, God, it was *supreme!*

Her decks crawling with heroes and heroines, Ivy League and Big Ten, East and Midwest united evermore, with a blast of exhaust The Green Nurd backs away in a wide arc, gathers speed, full astern, faster, faster!

Profanity in Spanish on the flying bridge! Profanity in English! Pablito and the Princetonian do not know how to reverse!

The far shore nears! Yells of alarm! Freighted with more than fifty kids, more than twenty tons of cargo, The Green Nurd backs damn-the-torpedoes into the pilings!

Shudders and splinters, she lurches, the engines are at last reversed, she gains momentum rapidly, full speed ahead upon the same doomed, damned course!

Another crisis on the bridge! Curses in Spanish! Curses in English! The wheel does not respond! The steering system has been jammed by impact!

Rebounding across the canal she bears down upon the dock, upon the paralyzed and uncoördinated crowd until, with atomic detonation *The Green Nurd* batters like a ram into the dock, through the dock, timbers flying, and plows head-on into the pilings! Her bow is stove, into her cabins rush the cruel waters! Her deck awash, The Modern Mariners submerged to their waists, *The Green Nurd* sinks, settles on the bottom, a tragic hulk, a derelict of destiny!

11

Jungle Jim Everglade Cruise: largest Indian trading post, plus Seminole village and alligator wrestling. Stop at world-famous chimpanzee farm. Acres of tropical gardens, colorful birds, hundreds of chimps, monkeys, baboons, alligators, crocodiles, tortoises and many other animals. Rest room on boat.

The beach was like something out of one of those current charming stories in which there has been a hydrogen war and the human race is about extinct and the last three survivors fag around looking for a fourth for badminton or something. Except that there weren't even three this afternoon. For miles I was the only sign of existence. It was a classic day, no clouds, and way far out on the bland blue face of the fat man a ship whispered smoke. I had been on the beach since early morning, sleeping mostly. It was a good, symbolic place to wind up, I thought, because life itself is sort of a beachathon: we lizard out of the undersea and species around in the sun for a short while until night falls and it is time to belly back again.

My suitcase stood beside me because I first planned to don a dress in a gas-station bique and take a bus into Miami and get a job as a dance-hall hostess or bet girl at the jai alai or something equally glamorous but finally I decided to call home, reversing the charges because I had only $12.21 including her last three dollars which Tuggle made me take, but I had no hunch who to call, my mother at the house or my father at the store. The thing was, I wasn't ready to start scavenging. I meant it when I said I was not going to use the world to ride after any damn brass rings.

So I swabbed on more tan oil and lay back on the towel and wondered what had happened to the kids. By now they had been six or eight hours on some road to somewhere. Had Tuggle found bliss with Quent? When she had left, crying because I was staying, her ride had promised to stop by the Imperador so she could see if his flag was still there. Maybe it had been, maybe they were together in Miami being married this minute or something. Was Ryder on his prosaic way north to South Nuxton, Mass., in the black Chevy? Was The Basil Demetomos Quarter: Dialectic Jazz reunited in the muddy, mutilated Mark XX and tooling toward Columbus, Ohio, or San Francisco? Had TV Thompson sold his Porsche and putzed off to Cuba? The aftermath of the wreck of *The Green Nurd* had been fairly awful. We had sloshed ashore from the hulk. Grown boys and girls wept. I think Basil wrote Ryder out a check for fifty-five thousand dollars but I'm not sure, that was just the rumor. Then everyone cut the sordid scene silently to pick up their bags and rides and start the trek home. But looked at objectively, there was no cause for collective guilt. We had tried to do a good deed. We had proved to ourselves we were basically sound and brave and pioneer. We had proved to ourselves that given cruel odds we would place our bets, given a colorful cause we would fight, given the right parade we would lead. And if we had flubbed, so? We had thrown into it the old college try without being rah-rah. Our trouble had been that of our time itself: bad navigation.

I was not alone any more. Down the beach three old ladies appeared and stuck chair backs in the sand and reclined to catch the sun. I did not mind them if they did not mind me. They were probably rich and widowed and lonely and spent every winter in Florida and had for three weeks been denied the beach while it was usurped by the younger generation. They wore big hats and dark glasses and sack swim suits and smoked and their skin was brown and oystery and their knees were like ears.

Thinking of money I also wondered if my $115 for a spring vacation in Lauderdale had been well squandered. In certain specific areas I had accomplished nothing.

"Travelling is a fool's paradise," to quote Ralph Waldo from "Self-Reliance," and "My giant goes with me wherever I go." How true. I still had no major. When I thought about it, however, it seemed to me what really mattered was not what you majored in, not *what* I would be but *who,* what *kind* of person I would develop into. And as far as I could tell none of the kids in the group had solved any of their problems either. BB-stackers are we all. O, well, *integer vitae* would be my future motto. And though I had gathered no data whatever on my inreach and outreach I really had a lyric tan.

The sun was passionate and I rubbed the warmth deeper into my arms and felt how plastic and young my skin was and how someday it would be wrinkled, like that of the old ladies, and suddenly I went on a death-kick. I couldn't help it. I had heard kids say that sooner or later everyone has his first intimation of mortality; that is, there comes a terrible instant when you know in your very bowels that *you* will die, that even *your* too, too solid flesh will melt. I had never had it. Now I really did. I turned cold. I touched myself all over. I shuddered with terror. Worms. I burst into tears in my towel. For a long while I was spastic on the sands. Then slowly the sun reblessed me. I was only nineteen. I had great groups of time left. I grinned at myself.

Incidently, I was preg. That's right, p.r.e.g. I'd been sure for five days. I had missed the boat by that much and I had always reached port right on schedule. Why hadn't I screamed for a shotgun? Because the marshy truth was that I hadn't the faintest who was the father, TV or Ryder or Basil, respectively and chronologically, or which one I really loved, or if the father and the one I loved would turn out to be identical. I had been carried away by Florida at the beginning, then when I had recovered my poise and morals and maturity, etc., it was too late. Besides, I had a brilliant mental picture of how each one of My Tropical Trio would react to The Shaft of paternity. TV would clap on a crazy hat, unfalcon his hands, and promote a coast-to-coast intercollegiate betting pool on the exact date and hour of arrival. Ryder would rise sportingly to his new obligations and disappear forever in detergent. Basil, his guidance system thrown utterly out of whack, would whiz spaceward and the nose cone of his genius would never be recovered. They were searchers, wonderful searchers, and I was *mad* for them; in other words I liked them tremendously; but to be honest I did not really *love* any one of them. TV had been my charity, Ryder my dream, Basil my project, but I would make none of them a sharp wife. I had already tried to change them, to make TV more responsible, Ryder less, and Basil more directional, and boys, I don't believe, are much improved by female tampering. *Let* Herbert Thompson, schizoid, phony, remarkable, make his mark upon the planet. *Let* Ryder have his efficiency, his conformity, his League attire; they also serve who only make home laundries. *Let* Basil, the cynic with a soul, the poet of the boxsprings, the hater looking for love, wander the earth like Diogenes, toting a string bass instead of a lantern. Yes, it was better and more selfless to make a gift of them to society as they were, unformed as yet, untrammeled, and unpredictable. That was a good deed I *could* do.

So, class, Merrit of the U had come to Lauderdale and won the Grand Prix de Sexe. All the other kids would be taking home souvenirs; post cards and swizzlesticks and baby crocodiles and menus and baskets and stuff; so would I. Travel is *supposed* to be broadening. You should have the message by now that I had decided to simply have my baby and not make a big production of it. Along with his three possible fathers, he would be my seven-pound offering to the century. I would certainly not pull anything baggy and abortive, nor would I be ridiculous and sit around in Core Living class spring term becoming gross as a dirigible. No, it was time I got out of the paperbacks and into life's hard covers. In a few minutes I would call my father and say hi, this is Merrit, I'm still in Lauderdale, the temperature down here is eighty, keeping it light and casual in order not to break up maudlinly. You are too young to be a grandfather but you are going to be and will you wire me enough money to make Carter City and is there room for me at the inn? I feel great and I can work at the store to pay board and room until the accouchement. I miss you and Mom and it would be fine to be home again among the chocolate malts and cosmetics and patent medicines and magazines, home again in The Most Beautiful Little City In The World By A Dam Site. Your daughter and her high IQ made a few mistakes down here, I went sort of morally berserk for three or four days due to my youth and Florida and inexperience and smalltown background, etc., some spastic, promiscuous things I never did before and never will again, I swear. And, Father and friend, I also swear, straight-arrow, if my coming home is acceptable, to next year enroll in some small, peaceful school and major in something and someday graduate and marry and be a *pillar*. I knew he would say okay and I could depend on him not to be Mickey Mouse.

I raised myself and stretched and lit an herb and stuck a hand into the sand and felt something and dug it up. It was a lost rubber sandal with a used Band-Aid stuck to the strap. Someone else had been wounded. The beach, except for the three old D.A.R. ladies and me, was still a wasteland. There I sat, 181226, a Daughter of the Cuban Revolution. Having my baby, I mused, might be the spiritual equivalent of going to fight in Cuba. I would be my own Green Nurd. I carried my own precious cargo. And another thing, by George, in my condition no one could call me an *Uncom*. Besides, to paraphrase Big Bill Shakespeare, the best pal English profs and teachers ever had, we owe God more than a death, we owe Him a *life*.

I made up my mind to call home in about ten more minutes, after the last of the sun had aced out on me. I was slightly exhausted and scared and lonely but also trembling with challenge and motherhood and mysticism. I would drop into the desolate Sand Crab, have a final beer in memory, then put in the call.

Incidently, I have never said anything about the etymology of my name, which is quite interesting. I am named after my Great-grandfather Merrit. I never met him, of course, because he died many years before I was born, but my father remembers him well as a boy. A young farmer, he had run away to enlist in a cavalry regiment and had fought through the Civil War and afterward married and settled down. I have seen his saber. In later life his hero was Mark Twain. He read every word Mark Twain had ever published and kept cats though he hated them because Mr. Clemens did and learned to play billiards. When he was a very old, bearded, but still very soldierly man, about seventy-five, he took an eccentric trip by himself on the train all the way from Carter City to New York City and while there happened to have a haircut in the Brevoort Hotel barbershop by a barber who *claimed* to have trimmed Mark Twain's mane on one of the great humorist's visits to New York and to have *saved* the sweepings, a few hairs of which he would be willing to sell in a small box for a large consideration. This was in 1916. My great-grandfather gave the barber all the money he had and returned home at once with his prize. That box and those few silver hairs were the dearest and proudest possession of his old age. He made a ceremony of showing them to everyone. One day he put the box on a table and opened it to show the contents to my father, who was then a Tom Sawyer-type boy of six. While my father was staring wide-eyed he suddenly had to sneeze and his sneeze blew the immortal Mark Twin's hairs into infinity. Frozen with awe at what he had done, certain he would get the most ancient and experienced spanking of his life, my father waited his punishment. After an almost Biblical minute his grandfather smiled and laid a gentle hand upon his head and closed the box and never again spoke of the matter in the two years left to him on this earth. When my father grew up he made up his mind—whether I was a girl or a boy—to name me Merrit. That is the kind of *sterling* guy he is.